SMALL CRIMES
IN THE BIG CITY

by

Steve Slavin

SMALL CRIMES IN THE BIG CITY

Published by
Fat Dog Books
California, USA

Fat Dog Books
ISBN: 978-0-9991370-7-9

Literature & Fiction/Contemporary/Short Story Collection
Printed in the United States of America

Visit our website at www.fatdogbooks.com

WARNING
The stories in this book are based on actual crimes committed by New Yorkers. They are presented here solely for your entertainment. Please do not even think about kicking the tires, let alone taking a test drive.

ACKNOWLEDGMENTS

Getting a short story collection published may be harder than being selected for the lead in a Broadway play, and certainly a lot less lucrative. The reason is very simple: short story collections don't sell. In fact, many bookstores refuse to stock them.

I have been extraordinarily fortunate in finding a publisher willing to take a chance. And now, three short story collections later, he is taking an even bigger chance with this book, a dozen short stories and a novella. Not only has Mike Stringer provided me with this opportunity, but he has very skillfully converted scores of stories into actual books.

Using a very light, but firm, editorial touch, Mike has smoothed out the rough spots, while managing not to alter the flow. But mostly, I appreciate the confidence he has shown in my writing.

One would think that after three books, we might stop before we flop. But now Mike is willing to take on an even greater literary challenge. Who is going to buy a bunch of short stories and a novella dealing with small crimes in the big city? Well, maybe we'll be able to convince everyone that "A Case of Stolen Identity" may actually be "the Great American Novella."

Two other people have also been extremely helpful. My old high school friend, Linda Sperling, was editing my stories even before I even conceived of trying to get them published as a collection. Linda is amazingly knowledgeable, and has generously provided several story ideas. A great story-teller in her own rite, she prefers the oral tradition.

Summer Hanford, another author with Fat Dog Books, is my web designer, as well as my ambassador to the world of high-tech communication. You can view her work on my website, tothecity.net. A fellow former fellow academic, she shares with me a jaundiced view of that world.

Another of my high school friends, Chuck Stickney, has not just made many helpful suggestions, but he suggested that I put my stories together into a collection. Now, four books later, neither he nor I had any idea things would get this out of hand.

Another author, Jacqueline Seewald, who has written more than a dozen novels, has generously shared her knowledge and expertise of the publishing world. Jacquie has kindly written reviews for each of my books.

I would also like to thank all my friends who provided story ideas or served as models for characters in these stories. Among them are Lillian Farber, Betty Lou Dorr, Arnie Schwartz, Len Friedman, Barbara Hanna, Serene Karp, Sergei Hershkoviki, and Sheila Tronn.

And finally, I'd like to thank my niece–and the family grammarian–Justine Zimiles, for her very helpful comments.

The heart and soul of short story publishing are the small literary magazines, virtually all of which accept submissions from unknown writers. They judge your work fairly, do not demand that you have a literary agent, and do not require that you be a "hot young author."

Nearly every short story in this book appeared in a magazine listed here. I want to thank each of their editors, not just for publishing my work, but for their helpful criticism and encouragement.

Entropy, Eskimo Pie, Fox Adoption Magazine, Gangway, Ravencagezine, Section 8, Short-Story.Me, Story Quilt, and The Literary Hatchet.

Ask any New Yorker which is the greatest city in the world and you know what they'll answer. I have lived here my entire life. The City has not only provided the settings, but the stories themselves. All I've done is write them down.

TABLE OF CONTENTS

Feeding the Hungry

1

You've probably heard stories about college girls who used to sneak their boyfriends into their dorm rooms after curfew? OK, I realize I'm dating myself by even knowing about this, but back in the days before the sexual revolution, we sometimes needed to be a little creative.

Not long after I graduated from college, I was dating a nun. I'm not putting you on—if you'll forgive my using a "sixties term."

As you know, very few nuns lived in college dorms. That's *right!* They lived in convents.

Theresa was in the Sisters of Charity. They were pretty strict but had a great collective sense of humor. Here's a brief sample:

Three nuns had taken a vow of silence. After ten years, Sister Mary was allowed to utter one sentence. When her turn came, Sister Mary said, "My porridge is lumpy."

Ten years later, Sister Bethany reported that, "My porridge is thin."

After still another ten years passed, Sister Patience, who happened to be the cook, finally had *her* turn: "I'm going to quit cooking if this bickering doesn't stop!"

If any of the sisters had an inkling of my intrusions, no one reported me. Maybe they were sound sleepers. But one night, when I showed up at the back door, Theresa was standing there, just shaking her head.

"*What?*" I asked, knowing the jig was up.

"Harry, you are a complete *schmuck!*"

I almost burst out laughing. Theresa had grown up in Brooklyn, just a few blocks from me. So, I knew how she'd picked up some of the lingo. Still, she *was* a nun.

"Did somebody *see* me?"

"*No!* Much *worse* than that!"

"So *tell* me already!"

"Mother Superior received multiple complaints. Someone had been leaving the toilet seat up."

2

Theresa and I knew each other when we were kids. Then she went to some out-of-town fancy Catholic College. I later heard that she had become a nun.

"What a *waste!*" I said to myself. Since we were thirteen or fourteen, I'd had. a crush on her—not that I ever got up the nerve to ask her out.

We ran into each other when we were in our early twenties. I was friendly with her brother Frank, who had invited me to a family barbeque. As soon as I saw her, I was in love all over again.

She wasn't wearing a habit or anything, although she still did have that angelic smile. We got into a conversation, and she told me the terrible news.

Shit! What a fuckin' *waste!*

She saw my expression and smiled. And I was lost.

What I didn't know at the time was that she had begun having doubts about her vocation. We agreed to keep in touch.

Then, once a month, we would meet for lunch. Lunch was safe, right? It wasn't a date.

Well, as you easily surmised, one thing led to another, and pretty soon I was making out with a nun in apartment house hallways, Central Park, and even once under the Boardwalk in Coney Island.

The next step was for her to sneak me into the convent. I knew that we were bound to get caught; in fact, that might have made the sex even more exciting.

But our relationship was probably doomed from the start. Theresa was an idealist, someone who was charitable to her core. And *me?*

Well, besides just being a regular guy wanting to have a good time, I suppose I hoped to live the Great American Dream—a pretty wife, a big home in the suburbs, and three or four very bright and happy children.

I mean, was there anything *wrong* with that dream? Theresa teased me for being so middle class. After she dropped out of the order and became a regular civilian, she still scorned material goods, while devoting her life to helping the poor.

So even if I hadn't forgotten to lower the toilet seat, it would have become very clear that Theresa and I were just not meant to be. But I hoped to always stay in touch, even though our lives grew further and further apart.

3

I began to wonder if I would ever see her again. But maybe a clean break was better. Let's *face* it: how much of a future could there be in dating a nun—or even an ex-nun? And yet, deep down, I knew I'd never meet another woman anything like her.

I now realized that her attraction was her essential goodness. A few years later, I was not surprised to hear that she was running a soup kitchen on the Bowery.

I decided to drop in on her, so to win brownie points I brought a shopping cart filled with dozens of fresh-baked cannoli. As soon as I rolled the cart through the door, she spotted me, dropped what she was doing and threw her arms around me.

I don't think I was ever happier. Then she looked at the boxes in the cart and guessed. "Cannoli?"

"You betcha!"

There were fifty or sixty people seated around tables. She asked a couple of assistants to place some cannoli on each table.

"Well, *thank* you, Harry! It sure beats opening cans of fruit cocktail!"

"The years have been kind to you, Theresa."

"I don't know about *kind*, but as you'll surmise, they have been quite interesting. Did you know I left the order?"

"I think I *did* hear something to that effect."

"Yeah! In fact, you can say that I've gotten remarried."

She saw my jaw drop. Quickly, she placed her hands on my shoulders and looked deep into my eyes.

"Harry, you will *always* be in my heart!"

"So, who's the lucky guy?"

She took my hand and walked with me to the back of the room. There was an older guy scraping bits of food from plates into a garbage pail. He was tall, slim, and had curly gray hair and a full beard.

"Tom, meet Harry."

"Glad to meet you, Harry. Where's Dick?"

Only guys named Tom, Dick, and Harry get the allusion instantaneously. He was definitely a kindred spirit.

"Tom, if I can't have her, then I'm glad it's *you*."

"Yeah, I'm like Allstate."

"I don't *get* it," said Theresa.

"You know their slogan: 'You're in good hands with Allstate.'"

She playfully punched him in the arm.

I really liked him right off. I could see why Theresa did. But, jeez, the guy was old enough to be her father. And indeed, I actually *knew* her father. They were probably about the same age, although Tom was certainly much more youthful.

After all the guests had left, I helped with the clean-up as Theresa brought me up to date with her life—and Tom's. The ex-nun and ex-priest had finally found happiness.

Tom had engaged in some activities that Cardinal Spellman had deemed unbecoming a priest. Spellman, an ardent supporter of our deep involvement in the Vietnam War, was particularly upset with reports about the vandalization of a couple of the local draft boards' records.

Tom never denied the rumors. He enjoyed describing himself as a de-flocked priest, since they *did* take away his flock. And as far as he was concerned, the Cardinal was a war criminal. Anyway, he had been dead for years.

"And what about *you*, Harry? Still counting money?"

"Yes, Theresa. As a matter of fact, I'm now a CPA and saving my clients millions in taxes they should be paying the government."

"Right *on!*" shouted Tom. "That money would have just fed the voracious war machine."

"Well, I hate to tell you guys, but I agree with you a hundred percent!"

"That's great to hear, Harry. I never *was* that clear on where you stood."

"Hey, I'm a lover, not a fighter."

They both laughed.

Then Tom said, "I surmise you were never in the service."

"Actually, I almost was. You might know that each draft board has a quota."

I noticed them glance at each other.

"Well, my draft board must have had a lot of guys who volunteered. So they would make up for any shortfall by drafting the youngest guys on their list. Now remember, this was back in the early sixties, just before the war heated up."

They both nodded.

"So when they finally called me in for a physical, I was just a couple of months short of my twenty-sixth birthday. And that was the cut-off."

Again, I saw them nodding. They seemed to know more about the draft than *I* did.

"Anyway, a friendly employee at my draft board explained that the military considered any guy who hit twenty-six 'untrainable'—you know, like being unable—or even unwilling—to follow orders, or to withstand the stresses of military training. I never did take that physical, and on my twenty-sixth birthday, I was officially untrainable."

Just then Theresa blurted out, "Did that include toilet training?"

Seconds later she and I were doubled over with laughter. Tom smiled, but he was clueless. Finally, Theresa told him that she would explain everything later.

"So Tom, perhaps in answer to your question as to whether I ever served in the military, the short answer would be 'No.' But a few years later, even *I* managed to engage in a very low level of passive resistance."

They were waiting to hear more.

13

"A few years ago, this poor guy from Internal Revenue paid me a visit—at home!"

"Welcome to the war-resisters' club," said Tom.

"I don't think I'm quite worthy of membership. All I had done was to deduct the federal telephone tax each month when I paid my phone bill."

"Of course!" said Theresa. "That tax was earmarked to help pay for the war!"

"Absolutely! So, this poor man—he must have been in his late fifties—climbed four flights of stairs to my apartment. He was huffing and puffing so much, I was afraid he would collapse. I insisted that he just sit and drink some water.

"While he was catching his breath, I began to feel very sorry for him. Here he was at this stage in his career, and he might just as soon have been working for a collection agency."

"Anyway, we went back and forth on the subject for about an hour. He kept insisting that I pay the tax, and I kept demanding that the government end the war.

Finally, he summed up the government's position. I had made my point. The IRS would now simply put a levy on my bank account. End of story."

"You should have asked him for an IRS official war-resister's certificate."

"Thanks, Tom!"

4

After the last guest left and we had tidied up, we sat down and they filled me in on their operation. They got most of their food from the federal government surplus food program, and most of the rest from restaurants. This was supplemented by what they could buy with a few thousand dollars a month in cash donations.

"So, the good news is that we can provide lunch and dinner three times a week," observed Theresa.

"And the bad news is the other fifteen meals you *can't* provide."

"Spoken like a man with the soul of an accountant," said Tom.

I realized just then how much I liked him, and how much I wanted to help the two of them expand their operations.

"May I make a suggestion?"

"Of course!" they both blurted out.

"OK, you know how forgiving the Church can be, especially to the rich?"

They both nodded, smiling.

"A few hundred thousand—or better yet, a few million—dropped onto the collection plate can sometimes go a long way."

Theresa and Tom were grinning.

"Now correct me if I'm wrong," I said, pausing for effect, "but don't you hand out receipts for your donors' contributions—whether in cash or in kind?"

"I think I see where this is going," said Theresa.

"Really?"

"Harry, you rascal! I always knew you were a sinner, but until now I had never realized that you were actually evil!"

"Hey, if the church can forgive the rich for *their* sins, then surely it can forgive the rest of us for sinning while feeding the poor!"

"And so, ex-Sister Theresa, we have the blessing of a 'de-flocked' priest to commit a minor sin for the greater good."

"So perhaps, Harry, we can rename our operation 'the Saints and Sinner's Soup Kitchen.' That might not only get the Church on our backs, but perhaps the IRS as well."

"Look, you guys worry about the Church and leave the worrying about the IRS to me."

5

Call me a cynic, but if there's one thing I've learned on my job it's that most Americans want to pay as little income tax as possible. Indeed, you don't need to be a CPA to figure *that* out.

The only problem is that a lot of those potential tax cheats would feel at least a little guilty—not just because cheating is illegal—but because it might even be immoral. My job is to not just keep them out of jail, but to even make them feel good about cheating Uncle Sam.

Through the late 1960s and early 1970s, a growing number of Americans opposed our involvement in the Vietnam War, and resented paying taxes to support that endeavor. So, a lot of my clients were receptive to what my colleagues and I called "creative accounting."

Deducting the federal telephone tax from your phone bill was highly symbolic, but it was pathetically insufficient to starve the government of funds needed to pay for the war. Regretfully, my fellow accountants and I were not sufficiently imaginative to devise anything more creative.

Although the Vietnam War had ended a few years ago, and the war-criminal-infested Johnson and Nixon administrations were no longer in office, perhaps more Americans still hated the federal government rather than loved it. So, most of us not only *want* to cheat on our taxes but feel justified in doing so.

Theresa and Tom were quite ready to provide their fellow citizens with another just cause for reducing their tax bills. Indeed, the Catholic Church and the IRS agreed that taxpayers were entitled to pay less tax if they helped feed the poor.

Like other charitable organizations, "Daily Bread" provides receipts for the cash and in-kind contributions they receive. But, adapting Jesus's miraculous feat of feeding multitudes of the poor with just a few loaves of bread, Tom and Theresa would now try to follow a more up-to-date business model.

6

After spending a few days working out my scheme, I arranged a sit-down with Theresa and Tom to get their reaction.

"Let us begin by agreeing that none of this will go beyond the three of us."

"This sounds serious!"

"It is, Theresa! It tests our very souls."

"Nothing personal, Harry, but do accountants *have* souls?"

"Thanks a lot, Father Thomas!"

"OK, gentlemen, let's get down to business."

"Since we need to keep everything secret, we won't be leaving a paper trail. But, I promise, my plan is very simple.

"Here's part one: When businesses make food donations, you can encourage them to list larger quantities of the bagels, desserts, tuna salad, and the canned goods than they actually provide."

"In other words," Tom observed, "they'll be getting larger tax deductions from the IRS."

"Correct."

"And that's legal?" asked Theresa.

"Was the war legal?"

"Point taken."

"Now, here's part two of the plan. It's a little bit iffy, at least from a legal standpoint."

Each shot me a very questioning look. Clearly, a little finagling with the food donations is not a very serious legal offense. If they ever got caught, they would be given a small fine at most and perhaps a stiff warning to never do it again.

"Remember the story of the miracle of the bread?"

"Of course!" replied Tom. "Jesus handed out a few loaves of bread to his disciples, who tore off small pieces and handed them to many hungry people. The bread kept multiplying and thousands of people were fed."

"So, Harry, your plan is to have our cash donations multiply like the bread?" asked Theresa.

"Hey, if it worked almost two thousand years ago, it might *still* work now."

"And if it does, it will be another miracle!"

"From your lips, Tom, to God's ears."

"So, here's how it will work: You know all those monetary contributions you get each year?"

"You mean the hundreds of thousands of dollars that pour in?"

They chuckled.

"Yeah, right Theresa! Soon you'll probably need to hire an accountant to help you keep track. And an investment advisor to get you the best return on your idle funds.

"Well, what if I told you guys that maybe you could be pulling in much larger monetary contributions?"

Just then a guest walked in the door.

"Hey, let's ask her where *she* invests her money," quipped Theresa.

"Hi Tom! Hi Theresa! I hate to drop in on you after hours, but I was wondering if you could help me out."

"Sure, Bernice! Would you like a couple of cans of baked beans or tuna to tide you over until Friday?"

"That would be great, Tom! You're an angel!"

Everyone smiled.

After Bernice left, Theresa got up to do a little more tidying up. As I helped her, I noticed that Tom remained seated. Maybe the poor guy was finally beginning to feel his age. On the other hand, *I* should be in that kind of shape when *I'm* as old as he is now.

7

The next evening we picked up where we had left off.

"OK Harry, we're very curious how you propose to dramatically raise our monetary contributions."

"Tom, I know that you guys are familiar with the concept of indulgences."

They smiled at each other.

"So correct me if I'm wrong, but an indulgence is the Church's forgiveness for having committed a sin. And it is granted—and I need to be careful here—in exchange for a substantial monetary payment."

"Well," answered Tom, "while the Church may phrase that somewhat more elegantly, your description is pretty close to the mark."

"Good! So then, what I'd like to propose is that "Daily Bread," with a genuflection to the Church, grant indulgences in the form of tax deductions."

18

"But we already *do* just that."

"Yes Theresa, but surely you can do that on a much grander scale."

'Exactly how much grander do you have in mind?"

"Oh, maybe doubling contributions over the next few months.

I'll give you a numerical example. Joe Schmo has been donating $100 a month, and each month you give him a receipt for that amount. Suppose you make him an offer: If he'll double his donation, you'll quadruple the amount on each receipt."

"Let me do the math," said Theresa. "Joe now gives us $200 and we give him a receipt for $800."

"Hey, maybe you picked the wrong vocation. You could still become a CPA."

"Thanks a lot!"

"Don't mention it!"

Then Tom observed: "This would easily work for cash contributions, but wouldn't the IRS notice that a contributor's deduction was twice the sum of his checks?"

"Yeah, if they actually looked. But their practice is to look mainly at the receipts from the charities rather than the charitable deductions claimed by taxpayers.

"The IRS knows that some charities inflate the value of the donations they receive, but most taxpayers probably inflate the value of the donations they make. So the IRS examiners figure a receipt from a charity is more reliable than the deduction claimed by a taxpayer."

"You know, Harry, this can certainly work to some degree with our donors, but over a year, maybe just a few hundred people give us more than, say, twenty-five dollars."

"That sounds about right," added Theresa.

"Well, that's a start. You can ask your contributors to help spread the word. But I've saved the best for last."

They looked at me expectantly.

"I just happen to have a few dozen clients who might be interested in making contributions to "Daily Bread" *if* you would be willing to provide them with inflated receipts. And better yet, some of the partners at my firm might want to help out as well, especially if *they* could take nice deductions for contributing to a good cause."

They glanced at each other. Then Tom suggested that they each sleep on it and try to reach a decision the next day.

8

I knew that neither of them was risk-averse, but would they want to take the chance of being prosecuted for tax fraud? On the other hand, I was counting on their anger with the government not just for the war, but for its centuries of oppression of the poor and minorities.

When I arrived at the soup kitchen that evening, they appeared rather subdued. Perhaps they had some remaining doubts about this entire enterprise. Were they really willing to take the risk of getting shut down, and leaving all their guests in the lurch?

As I approached, the two of them stood there, their faces expressionless. Then, bowing their heads, they raised their fists, just like Tommie Smith and John Carlos did on the victory stand at the 1968 Mexico City Olympics.

I was overjoyed! Not only were they in, but they appeared as defiant as Smith and Carlos in *their* protest. It was their way of saying "Fuck you!" to our corrupt and murderous government. I got their message loud and clear without their having said a word.

The three of us hugged, and Tom declared, "All for one and one for all!"

Then I handed them a check and asked for a receipt for the amount on the check. They each gave me a questioning look.

"Look, you'll want some receipts to match the amount on the checks. Besides, don't you want your accountant to be above suspicion?

"Over the next few days you'll be getting some checks in the mail from new donors. Each will mention my name. So could you double or even triple the amount of their donations on their receipts."

"It will be our pleasure!" replied Tom.

"Oh, and one more thing. For the folks I send to you who donate cash, could you quintuple the amount on their receipts?"

"Of course!" said Theresa. "It's like the long-honored practice of merchants who don't charge sales tax on purchases paid for with cash. I believe that every service station in New York has that generous policy."

"Cash is good!" I replied. After all, every piece of our currency contains the statement, 'In God we trust.' And as some of our fellow citizens have added, all others pay cash.

"Oh, and speaking of cash, here are a few donations my clients just made." I handed them each two envelopes.

"Holy *shit!*"

"Isn't that a little blasphemous—even for an *ex*-nun to say!"

"Not for *this* donation!"

"So how much will the receipt be for?"

"Two thousand five hundred dollars!"

"Thank you, Theresa! That's very generous."

Then Tom piped up, "Oh Lordy! It looks like Alfred Goldfarb has just earned himself a five-thousand-dollar deduction!"

"Wow! Now, if our guests don't have *bread*, we can let them eat *canoli!*"

"Yes, Tom! And to paraphrase the American Revolution War naval hero, Captain John Paul Jones, 'We have just begun to cheat!'"

9

One evening when I dropped by, I found Theresa all alone in the store. The assistants had left for the day and Tom, who had not been feeling well lately, had stayed home all day.

"You know, Harry, this might be a good chance for us to talk."

I gave her a quizzical look, not sure what was coming next.

"Oh, don't worry! It's just something that I've wanted you to know. Let me start by asking if you're familiar with the "Underground Railroad.""

"Of course! It was a network to help escaped slaves get themselves smuggled out of the South to their freedom in the North."

"Well, when I volunteered to help draft dodgers—and even some military deserters—I met Tom. He was one of the organizers."

"That doesn't surprise me at all."

"You really like him, don't you?"

"You know I do! He's fun, he's modest, he has great ideals, and he's even almost as good-looking as *I* am! What's *not* to like?"

She gave me a playful jab in the arm. I pretended to double over in pain.

"You know, Harry, there might be a future for you in professional wrestling."

"Seriously, Theresa, Tom has been leading an amazing life. If the Feds had known even a fraction of the shit he's done, they'd have given him the electric chair.

"By the way, there's something I need to tell you."

I could see that she was very curious.

"You know, when I first laid eyes on him, my first thought was, How could she *go* for such an old guy?"

We both smiled.

"Right! And now I know!"

"I believe you do, Harry. Still, I want you to know what Tom and I did, not all that long ago, working on the modern-day Underground Railroad."

I waited, watching her gather her thoughts.

"Tom's main job, besides planning and organizing many of our operations, was driving to the Canadian border with a couple of young men who were his 'nephews.' They were ostensibly on the way to a family birthday party or maybe a wedding. Tom would vary the routine, sometimes heading for

Toronto, Montreal, or even Vancouver. Remember that even a few years ago, the customs officials of both countries did not use computers, which might have helped them keep better track of who crossed the border lately."

"And what was *your* job?"

"Would you believe it was that of the blushing bride?"

"You're putting me on! "

"Moi?"

"Yeah, *vous!*"

"Harry, I've lost track of how many times I've gotten married—not to mention how many times I've seen Niagara Falls, for that matter."

"So, it would be fair to assume that you and Tom did not go there on *your* honeymoon."

"That would *indeed* be a fair assumption."

"Did you or Tom ever have any close calls?"

"Probably. You could never be sure. When the young men were asked to show their draft cards, *that* was kind of a tip-off. On the other hand, it was probably just a random thing they did."

"I would have been scared shitless!"

"Hey, Tom and I both were. The thing was, of course, that if either of us got caught, we'd have been facing long prison sentences. Tom kidded me about that, saying that he probably didn't have all that long to live anyway."

"Lovely."

10

As our scheme took hold, Daily Bread began providing lunch and dinner a fourth day each week and there was hope it would eventually be able to fully live up to its name. And with federal government surplus food shipments increasing, we added a food pantry to our operation.

We were indeed duplicating Jesus's bread distribution miracle, aided as we were by modelling our contribution plan on the old-time Church indulgences. And all this made possible by a former nun, a de-flocked priest, and a creative accountant.

My thirty-third birthday was approaching, and I spent increasing amounts of time thinking about what I had done with my life, and what I still hoped to accomplish. I'm sure its symbolism was not lost on Tom and Theresa.

I remembered a cartoon which pretty much summed up my thoughts. This poor soul in a business and clutching a heavy sample case was standing nervously before the Pearly Gates, waiting to learn if he would be admitted to heaven. Saint Peter was poring over a ledger. Finally, he looked up and asked, "Salesman of the year in 1971? That's it?"

I was confident that if, even five minutes from now, I were to find myself in that man's place, I would have a better shot at getting into heaven. Perhaps Saint Peter would be impressed with my CPA. But I was certain that the assistance I had provided to Daily Bread, however dubious its legality, would be much more helpful.

But hopefully, the greater part of my life still lay ahead of me. Then I thought of Tom, trying to imagine all the amazing things he had done. And how, decades from now, my accomplishments would stack up against his. As I did this, I began to realize that this man was truly a living saint.

You could not help but love him. So, I easily understood how *he*—and not *I*—had ended up with such a wonderful woman. Did I still *love* her? Of *course!* I knew that I would love her until the day I died.

But Tom truly deserved her, and I was very happy that everything worked out for them. And better yet, in just the last couple of months, I had certainly added to their happiness— and to my own as well.

Indeed, for the first time in my life, I began to understand the proverb: To give is better than to receive. I don't think there had been any time in my life when I was happier—with the possible exception of when, in 1955, the Brooklyn Dodgers finally beat the New York Yankees in the World Series. That miraculous event convinced me—and perhaps every person in Brooklyn—that all things were possible.

I asked myself: Am I truly happy? Well, to be completely honest, I certainly would have greatly preferred the Hollywood ending, where the boy ends up with the girl. But to have had that ending, to start the boy should have never let her go.

And yet, to see her so happy—probably a lot happier than *I* could have ever made her—well, that makes *me* happy. Tom is really perfect for her, although I laughed to myself thinking, I bet she could've gotten someone a little younger.

These last few months, helping them answer their life's calling, I began to recognize—if I was not being too presumptuous—my *own* calling. Even accountants can contribute to a great eternal plan.

Theresa and Tom took me out for dinner on my birthday. They had become my closest friends. Tom mentioned that his *own* birthday was just a few weeks away. It would be "the big six-oh!"

"Tom," I can't believe all the *things* you've done with your life."

"You know, Harry, I must confess that your own life has been an inspiration to *me!*"

"Really?"

"Of course! For me, God was always there to guide me. And if I may be so presumptuous, God has also always been there to guide Theresa."

"Hey, I think you guys should give yourselves a lot of credit. I'm sure the two of you are familiar with the adage, God helps those who help themselves."

"Of course we are," replied Theresa. "That said, the individual still has to go out and *do* it."

"Harry, just consider how much you've changed during these last few months. Think of how much more you've enabled us to help our guests."

"You know what, Tom? I am forced to concede that you and Theresa are right. So I hope you remembered to order a birthday cake."

As if on cue, the waiters emerged from the kitchen singing "Happy Birthday," and most of the diners joined in.

25

11

It might have been just my imagination, but Tom seemed to be dragging ass more and more. It made me wonder what I'd be like when I was *his* age. And what I'd be doing and who I'd be with when I reached the big six-oh.

I asked Theresa if she and Tom had any plans for *his* birthday.

"Funny you should ask. I was just thinking about throwing a surprise party in the store."

"That sounds perfect!"

"I'm glad to hear that. I'd like to invite not just his family members and old friends, but also all of our regular guests."

"How can you keep it a surprise?"

"Well, there's the old trick—or should I say 'tricks?'"

"And what would *those* be?"

"Well, we can hold it a week before his birthday."

"I *like* that! It will catch him off guard."

"And we'll keep him out of the store when we're setting up."

"How would we do *that?*"

"With my secret weapon: Father Timothy."

"How do I *know* that name? Wait! Did he have something to do with damaging some records at the local draft boards?"

"Bingo!"

"Anyway, the two of them have not gotten together for some time, so Timothy agreed to come over to our apartment on Friday the 20th in the late afternoon. I'll open a bottle of sacramental wine and suggest that the two of them hang out there while I go to the store to get dinner started. Then, if they came over toward the end of dinner, say around seven p.m., maybe they could help clean up."

"Sounds like a plan."

"In the meanwhile, I've got a list of about a hundred people I want to invite—in addition to our regular guests."

"Can the store hold that many people?"

"Well, not all of them will be able to come, so there should be enough room. The main thing is to invite Tom's friends and family, and to surprise the shit out of him."

"So the dinner guests won't know about the surprise party until they get there, and the friends and family will be sworn to secrecy."

"Correct!"

"So Father Timothy will be a key player."

"Yes! And I know he'll enjoy every minute of it. The two of them go back a long, long way."

On Friday, May 20th, at four minutes after seven, the lookout spotted Tom and Timothy coming down the street. She could tell even from fifty yards that they might be just a wee bit tipsy. She rushed into the store and gave Theresa the high sign.

Theresa announced to everyone that Tom was about to walk in. By now everyone knew that it was his birthday. As soon as the door opened, and the two of them stumbled in, everyone yelled, "*Surprise!*"

Tom blinked a couple of times, perhaps checking to see if he was awake. Timothy put his arm around him and announced: "The birthday boy has arrived!"

Theresa rushed up to Tom and gave him a long, deep kiss. Everyone cheered. Then Tom looked around, laughing as he pointed at each of his old friends and his brother, his sister, his cousins, and even his favorite aunt.

Then, one-by-one, they approached him for a hug and wished him a happy birthday. Then he needed to sit down for a while. He looked exhausted.

Theresa stood behind him, her hands resting on his shoulders. Tom clearly needed a break, so she introduced Father Timothy, and asked him to tell everyone about the good old days.

For the next half hour Timothy told anecdote after anecdote, some of them dating back to their seminary days. He had Tom smiling and nodding, while he himself basked in all the attention.

Then a huge birthday cake was wheeled in and placed in front of Tom. After a rousing "Happy Birthday" was sung, Tom asked Timothy if he had enough wind left to help him blow out the candles. Together, they were certainly up to the task, as everyone cheered.

Then the crowd started chanting, *"Speech! Speech! Speech! Speech!"* until Tom held up his arms in surrender.

"If it's OK with everyone, I'd like to remain seated. I hope you all can hear me."

"Tom, we hear yuh and we love yuh!" yelled Bernice.

"Thank you, Bernice! Unlike my dear fellow seminarian, I promise to be very brief.

"To see all of you in this room is like viewing a vast photo album of my entire life. Because you are the most important people—to me, at least—on this planet. Indeed, you *are* my life.

"Were I as eloquent as Father Timothy, I would thank each of you for enriching and giving meaning to my life. So please, let me pause for a minute or two, to let you imagine how I would be thanking you.

"Now, let me close with the immortal words of a man I always greatly admired, New York Yankee great, Lou Gehrig. 'I consider myself the luckiest man on the face of the Earth.'"

I shuddered, remembering that Gehrig died months after he uttered those words. Only now did I realize just how ill Tom was, and how gently and considerately he was bidding farewell to everyone in the room.

The Larcenous Mrs. Lewis

My name is Jim Lewis, and I have never been married. In fact, my longest relationship lasted just two months. And that one ended during the administration of President Jimmy Carter.

Yeah, I know what you're thinking: How old could this guy *be*? Well, you know that policy that President Clinton recently started with the military—"Don't ask; don't tell"? I *love* it! And the ladies do tell me I look good for my age. If you've even glanced at the personal ads, the chances are you've come across some like this one: Youthful, very successful businessman, late forties, looking for very attractive college educated woman, 20-29, for a serious relationship.

I didn't write this ad, but the guy who did could have been my twin. Because my ideal woman would be beautiful, smart, and in her twenties. Now I'm not claiming that women like that are busting down my door, but on the other hand, why settle? Older guys like me often have trouble adjusting to the title, Ms., which has largely replaced Miss and Mrs. Back in the day, when women married, they proudly took not just their husband's surname, but often his first name as well. For example, Miss Sheila Schlockowitz was magically transformed into Mrs. William Prescott. But on the downside, Miss Larisa Karamazov became Mrs. Culpepper Exum, the third. Not that any of this really matters, since I am not exactly marriage material.

I mean, I like attractive women—the younger the better—but I don't expect to hear wedding bells any time during the next forty or fifty years. So, you can imagine my surprise when credit card bills began to arrive in my mailbox that were addressed to Mrs. James Lewis. Clearly, there had been some mistake.

Whatever else might be said of me, I am not exactly the marrying kind. It follows, then, that there *is* no Mrs. James Lewis living with me. You're welcome to check for yourself, but please call first, because my apartment is usually a mess.

Mrs. James Lewis had run up nearly two hundred thousand dollars of debt on a wide array of bank and department store credit cards. When I finally began calling some of these institutions, it was explained to me that a Mrs. James Lewis of 149 West 9th Street was the owner of these cards. When the woman from the credit department at Macy's told me that I was legally responsible for my wife's debts I blurted out, "*Wife!* Listen, lady, I can't even get a *date!*" She hung up on me, perhaps thinking that I was hitting on her.

The bills kept coming and I grew more and more desperate. I finally decided to hire a matrimonial lawyer. The first thing I told her was that I was not now, nor ever *had* been married. "Excuse me, Mr. Lewis, but am I missing something here? My practice is exclusively matrimonial law. Perhaps you would be better served by engaging a dating service."

"Let me start from the beginning." For the next hour I poured my heart out to her. From time to time, she would ask a question. And when I finally finished, she provided an excellent summation. "Mr. Lewis, you are the victim of credit card fraud. But you are not legally liable for these debts because you are not married to the person who committed this fraud."

"So. I'm in the clear?"

"Well, not completely. First of all, your credit has certainly been ruined. And second, some of the creditors may take legal action against you."

"What can I do?"

"You can go to the police. Or, you can engage a private investigator. Or possibly both."

"What would you advise?"

"Well, why not go to the police first. And if you're still not satisfied, I can give you the phone number of a private investigator who specializes in this area."

I wasn't sure if I felt better or worse after talking to the lawyer, but her advice did sound pretty good. The next day I walked over to the 6th Precinct, which was just around the corner. After an hour's wait, I got to explain my predicament to a detective.

He told me that he would share this information with detectives who dealt with consumer fraud, and that, if I really wanted to pursue this, he could set up an appointment for me with someone in that unit. In the meantime, he suggested that I make copies of all the bills I had received.

A week later I met with Detective Michael Riley of the Consumer Fraud Squad. After looking over all the bills, he smiled at me. "Well, Mr. Lewis, I have some good news and some bad news."

Right! The good news would be that I was married to a beautiful woman half my age, and the bad news that she had bankrupted me. What he actually said was that I was just the latest of a series of victims of a woman who had been running this scam for years. So I was definitely not legally responsible for all these bills. In fact, he would see to it that all the credit card companies and department stores were informed of this, and that my credit would be fully restored.

And the bad news? Although they had had dozens of excellent leads, they still had not been able to catch this person. "Well at least can you explain to me how she had been able to get all these credit cards without my knowledge?"

"*That* I can do! She must have filed a change-of-address card with your local post office. All mail for Mrs. James Lewis of 149 West 9th Street was redirected to a post office box."

"OK, so that explains why I wasn't alerted while she was running up these bills."

"Exactly."

"But why did I suddenly start getting the bills about a month ago?"

"Well, after six months, the change-of-address order expires. The post office assumes that the addressee has informed his or her friends and family of the address change."

"So let me see if I understand this. This woman applied for credit as Mrs. James Lewis, filed a change-of-address card with the post office, and ran up huge credit card debts. Wow, that's unbelievable!"

"Not to *us*, it isn't."

"Is there anything else I can do?"

"As a matter of fact, there is. Try to think of anyone you know—even a distant acquaintance—who might have done this. Very often the victim actually knew the person committing the fraud—a spurned lover, a jealous friend or relative, an old enemy or rival. You'd be surprised how many people you might have pissed off."

"Well, I can't think of anyone off-hand, but I'll go through my address book as soon as I get home."

"Good! In the meanwhile, there are several things we can do on *our* end. Why don't you give me a call in, say, about ten days?"

Ten days later, when I called Detective Riley, I hoped he had had better luck than I did. My search had not turned up even one person who might have done this to me. He had had a little more success.

"We know from experience that when the scammer files a change-of-address card, she has the mail forwarded to a post office box. Each time she runs a new scam, she opens a different box. So we went to the postmaster in your local post office to find out where Mrs. James Lewis' mail was being forwarded. The Postmaster told us that the scammer had a box in that post office.

"We asked to see if she had any mail. There was a pile of credit card bills, all addressed to Mrs. James Lewis. The envelopes had been postmarked between forty to sixty days ago."

"Why wasn't she picking up the mail?"

"That's a good question. She knew that the credit card companies and department stores must have been getting wise to her, and she may have even suspected that the police were watching to see who was taking mail out of her post office box."

"Were you?"

"No. We don't have the manpower. And even if we did— we probably would have been weeks too late to catch her.

"And there was another thing. She must have known that six months after a change-of-address card is filed, the post office stops forwarding the mail. That's why, six months into her scam, you suddenly began getting all those bills."

"She really had that all figured out."

"Let me tell you, your 'wife' is one smart lady."

"Yeah, thanks a lot!"

"Wait, there's more! We opened each of the envelopes we found in the post office box. Would you believe that she had been making the minimum payment—about ten or fifteen dollars—every month?"

"Oh, I get it! As long as she did this, she could eventually max out each credit card."

"Right you are, Mr. Lewis."

"Boy, Mrs. James Lewis has a much better head for numbers than her husband."

"Oh, and there's one more thing. When you apply for a post office box, you are required to list not just your old address, but your new one. So even if you're having your mail forwarded to a post office box, you still must provide your new home address."

"I guess that makes sense," I said. "In case there's any problem with your post office box—if you didn't pay your rent on it, or maybe you weren't collecting your mail, the post office could get in touch with you."

"That is correct, Mr. Lewis. So, are you ready to hear what new address she put down for herself?"

"What was it?"

"Would you believe 149 West 9th Street?"

"That's *my* address!"

"I know. Usually the scammer will give a fictitious address, so we're thinking that, as a joke, she used yours. Think about it... she files a change-of-address card, she wants her mail forwarded from 149 West 9th Street to her post office box, and then she lists her current home address as the place she's moved from."

"That makes no sense!"

"Well, I guess maybe to her, listing your address twice was a joke. But when we catch her, we can ask her about it."

"So how will you catch her?"

35

"We're working with the postal inspectors. She's done this more than a dozen times, and she'll probably keep doing it. They are alerting the clerks in every post office in Manhattan who handle box applications to be on the lookout.

"We'll also continue to work with the credit card companies and the department stores, but in the past, neither has been very helpful."

I liked Detective Riley, but I didn't really expect to hear back from him. About a month later when my phone rang around 5:00 p.m., I braced myself for still another telemarketer.

"Mr. Lewis?"

"Yes?" I answered warily. At least the guy did not have a foreign accent, but I just knew his next words would be, "How are you today?" At which point I would slam down the receiver. So, you could imagine my shock when instead, the man said, "Your wife has been found!"

For several seconds I had no idea who this was or what he was talking about. And then it hit me! "Detective Riley? That is fantastic news!"

"For you *and* for us!"

"How did you catch her?"

"Well, it's kind of an interesting story. If you have time, why don't you drop by tomorrow afternoon, say about two? There's another detective I'd like you to meet."

"Great! See you then."

When I entered his office, Detective Riley shook hands with me and introduced me to Detective Johnson. She was tall, had long, very straight black hair that hung to her shoulders, and what I would call movie star looks. As we shook hands, her grip was strong. Then I noticed the wedding band on her other hand. When my eyes moved back up to her face, she smiled as though she could read my mind.

"Detective Johnson conducted the investigation, and thanks to her, we have finally apprehended the celebrated 'Mrs. James Lewis.'"

"Mr. Lewis, let me tell you right off that your 'wife' was something of an old friend of our unit. She is a career criminal.

36

In cases such as this one, we look for patterns or connections. Now we knew, of course, that 'Mrs. James Lewis'—using various aliases—had been pulling this scam for decades and had never been caught. Many of her 'husbands' have been in touch with us over the years. And while there have been other credit card scammers, none has been doing this for so long."

"Well, from what I've learned from Detective Riley, the scam works for no more than six months, so that means she's done this to a lot of guys."

"That's right. Now we were painfully aware that she's never been caught. So then we asked ourselves: What kind of scam would she have been working before this one? Perhaps she had been caught doing something else. That way, we'd know who we were looking for."

"Let me see if I'm following. If she's a career criminal, maybe before this she used to rob banks or something."

"That's a very interesting theory," said Detective Riley. "Because that's exactly what she *had* been doing."

"She went into banks and gave the teller a note saying that she had a gun?"

"Well," said Detective Johnson, "she was a little more sophisticated than that. What she did was walk into a bank, ask to see an officer, and tell him that she wanted to open an account. Now are you ready for the really interesting part? She said that she had started a business and needed to deposit $10,000 in cash. And that was quite a lot of money back in the late 1940s."

"Are you serious? That's almost 50 years ago! How *old* is this woman?"

"Maybe almost old enough to be your grandmother, Mr. Lewis."

"There goes my dream of having been married to a beautiful woman."

"Well, she certainly *was* a beautiful woman in her day. And she's really quite nice looking for a woman in her early eighties," said Detective Johnson.

"So how did she scam the bank?"

"She explained that she needed deposit slips for her account, because she would be making a large number of deposits during the next few weeks. But it used to take the banks about a month to have deposit slips printed for new accounts. So how, then, would she be able to deposit all this money?

Luckily the officer had an idea. He would assign her an account and provide her with a few hundred deposit slips. Each slip would have her account number printed on it. But would it be OK if the name of her business did not appear at the top of the slip? Of course it would be OK! And do you know *why*, Mr. Lewis?"

"I don't have a clue."

"OK, let's just back up a minute. The bank officer really wants her business. So he's willing to cut corners. When a customer opens a new account and wants to deposit money, he or she fills out a blank deposit slip that is found on the tables in the bank. Then the customer takes the slip and the cash or checks to be deposited to a teller."

"If I'm following, these deposit slips have no account numbers printed on them."

"Bingo! You're catching on fast," said Detective Johnson.

"So every morning she goes into the bank and places a few of her printed deposit slips on each table, and then leaves. Customers who have new accounts, or have forgotten to bring their deposit slips, will fill out one of her slips. And virtually no one will notice the printed account number at the bottom of the slip."

"That is amazing!"

"And when the teller puts through the deposit slip, the money goes into the scammer's account. Because the bank's computer reads the printed deposit number—and not what the customer has written on the deposit slip."

"So how did she get caught?"

Detective Johnson continued. "Her scam would work for just a month, because when depositors got their statements, they noticed that some of their deposits weren't recorded—and their balances were too low. By then our friend had withdrawn all the money out of her account—in cash.

"She may have even known that when a bank got scammed, its officers wouldn't bother to warn the officers of other banks. I guess nobody wants to look dumb."

"But they did report this to the police, of course," added Detective Riley.

"Right," agreed Detective Johnson. "And the police then visited every bank and warned them about her. One day, when she tried to open an account, an alert bank officer called the police. The tip-off was that she wanted to deposit $10,000 in cash."

"So then she went to prison?"

"She was sent away for eight years," answered Detective Riley.

"Then how did you make the connection between the bank scams and the credit card scams?"

"Well," said Detective Johnson, "it was a combination of deductive logic, trial and error, and just dumb luck. You see, we were obviously looking for a woman. And then we thought, she's pretty slick. Maybe she's a little older, a little more experienced.

"So far, so good. Then, another detective suggested that we look at some of the older scammer cases. We figured that since she was working with credit cards, maybe before that she had run some kind of banking scam."

"So how did you finally make the connection?"

"Well, that was plain dumb luck."

"Really?"

"Are you ready for this?"

"I guess."

"The woman we were looking for was actually living in your building. So all this time, she was hiding in plain sight."

"That is truly amazing! But how were you able to figure this out?"

"She made two mistakes. First, as you know, she listed 149 West 9th Street as her current address on the change-of-address form she gave to the post office. And second, she didn't bother to change her name. So when we checked the names on the list we compiled of old-time bank scammers, and then checked it against your apartment house directory, we had a match."

"*Wow!* That is truly impressive detective work! Can you tell me who she is?" The detectives looked at each other. After Detective Riley nodded slightly, Detective Johnson smiled and said, "Well, this may come as a shock, but she's actually your next-door neighbor."

"What? Do you mean old lady Fletcher?"

The detectives burst out laughing. "You are right on the money—so to speak," said Detective Riley.

"Oh my God! Would you believe that she actually used to flirt with me?"

"So you didn't flirt back?" asked Detective Riley.

"Yeah, right! I was always polite to her, but I'm looking for a woman half my age—"

"Rather than one twice your age?" asked Detective Johnson.

"Exactly!"

"Well, Mr. Lewis, maybe if you had been more receptive to her advances, you might have made an honest woman out of her."

The Great American Term Paper

1

We've been waiting for more than two centuries for someone to write The Great American Novel. There have been countless very, very *good* novels, but none that was truly great.

But The Great American Term Paper? That's an entirely different story.

That story began in Brooklyn almost forty years ago. Known mainly for its rundown Hebrew school, the Avenue R Temple was a veritable bar mitzvah mill. Eleven and twelve-year-old boys would attend a couple of two-hour classes every week to learn just enough Hebrew to read a few lines of Torah at their bar mitzvahs. And though Rabbi Steinbach extended an open invitation to Shabbos services to every bar mitzvah boy, almost none of us ever took him up on his offer.

Many of the temples around the city held singles dances to raise money. They were advertised primarily in *The New York Post*, aka *"The Jewish Daily Post,"* largely because nearly all their columnists and readers happened to be Jewish.

These dances were usually held on Saturday night after Shabbos had ended, but the Avenue R Temple had theirs on Sunday afternoon. The teenagers and young adults who attended were primarily from our neighborhood.

I had much better things to do than go to these dances. Just a couple of blocks from the temple was Kelly Park, where you could spend the entire day playing basketball, handball, stickball, softball, and even tennis (if you shelled out fifteen bucks for a permit).

My friend, Ira, was planning to attend the dance that coming Sunday and invited me to come along. I agreed to go only if it was raining.

"Dan, don't you want to meet a nice Jewish girl?"

"Maybe I can meet one at Kelly Park."

"Sure. But your chances are a lot better at the dance."

"OK, I'll see you if it rains."

2

The sun woke me up that morning and I arrived at the park just when it opened. I had such a good time, I even skipped lunch. Around five o'clock, I stopped by the Avenue R Temple. There, in the lobby of the Hebrew School, I saw Ira seated behind a table, chatting with a couple of girls.

I felt a little self-conscious in my torn jeans and sweaty tee shirt. Ira called me over and introduced me. While the four of us were chatting, I could hear the music in the gym downstairs. As they were leaving, Ira began to smile.

"Dan, are you wondering why I'm sitting out here, instead of going downstairs?"

"You're a mind-reader!"

"Indeed I am."

Just then, three more girls came up the stairs and into the lobby.

"Girls, would you like to sign our mailing list?"

They came over to the table and signed Ira's list. After they left, Ira burst out laughing. "This is like shooting fish in a barrel."

"Are you working for the Temple?"

"No Dan, I'm working for *me*."

"What are you going to do with the list?"

"Well, I have two alternatives. I can use their names for my mailing list when I run my *own* dance."

"Or?"

"Well, you see those check marks?"

"Holy *shit!*"

"Yeah, Dan, those are the ones I'll call up for dates."

"So the Temple doesn't know what you're doing?"

"Well, Mr. Brownstein sort of does. I told him I was watching the lobby."

"He believed you?"

"Don't I look like an honest guy?"

3

When we entered Brooklyn College that fall, the school offered just a few computer courses. Ira took them and then continued studying on his own.

"I'm telling you, Dan, computers will eventually take over the world."

"Yeah, but in the meantime, maybe you should think about how you're going to make a living."

It would be another twenty years before Ira would be proven right. The advent of PCs was the first step. Still, in the mid'80s, PCs cost over three thousand dollars (or about double that in today's dollars), and all they were really good for was word processing.

But by the new millennium, most Americans were on the Internet, and everything had changed. Ira, who ran a small computer repair business, was ready to make his big move.

"Dan, how would you like to go into business with me? With your brains and my creativity, we could go far."

I was an English Professor at Brooklyn College, newly-divorced, and struggling with child support payments. The City University paid fairly well, but I knew that even teaching every summer I would never earn nearly enough.

When Ira outlined his business plan, my first question was: Is that *legal?*

"Wrong question, Dan." He paused for effect. "The right question?" Again, the meaningful pause. "Can we get away with it?"

In a nutshell, the plan was to run a nationwide contest for college students that we would call The Great American Term Paper Contest. All college students were eligible. They could e-mail us their best term papers, and would be eligible for a range of monetary awards. First prize would be $10,000, and the title, author of that year's Great American Term Paper. There would be second, third, fourth, and fifth prizes, with lesser financial rewards.

But perhaps a more important set of rewards—there would be one hundred honorable mentions. Each recipient would receive a frameable certificate—something nice to list on applications to grad school, law school, business school—or even medical school.

Students could enter the contest as many times as they wished, sending a one-dollar entry fee for each paper through PayPal, an online startup. Very anxious to introduce its services to all those college students, the company would provide its services to us for free.

Who would judge the term papers? I had access to an army of interns who would receive college credit for their labor. They would do all the initial screening, eliminating over ninety-five percent of the submissions. The final decisions would be made by a panel of English professors, who would be paid small honorariums—a euphemism for chump change—but a very useful listing on their CVs.

"So, Ira, I'm guessing that if enough students send in their papers, we can finance the prize money with their entry fees."

"You see, Dan, you're just as smart as I always thought you were."

Then, reading my mind, he added, "But you have another question, possibly one about how we're going to get the word out to millions of college students."

"Won't that cost a tremendous amount of money?"

"It would indeed, if *we* had to pay for it."

"So, what's your plan, Kemosabe?" (If you're as old as we are, you'd remember that that's what Tonto used to call the Lone Ranger. While many of us assumed it meant 'friend,' it seems to have actually meant 'old schrub.')

"My plan, Tonto, is to send a press release to 5,000 college newspaper editors. Our contest will be big news to them—and to their millions of readers. If we can create a huge buzz, then a lot of students will enter the contest."

4

Over the next few weeks, we fleshed out our plan. There would be follow-up letters to the college newspapers from "students" who had entered the contest. We would send press releases to scores of daily newspapers, as well as smaller papers in college towns. Student interns would be lined up, and our panel of distinguished professors assembled.

As Ira observed, once a bandwagon starts rolling, everybody and his brother wants to jump on. And pretty soon, *our* bandwagon started to roll.

Still, I had my doubts. Ira's plan was working, but I didn't see how we would be making very much money unless we received hundreds of thousands of dollars from entry fees. But Ira said the real money would be made once the contest *really* took off, probably after the first year.

Our press release and letters were printed in hundreds of college papers, and we managed to assemble a panel of respectable, if not quite distinguished English professors. PayPal was delighted to see the trickle of payments from college students become a flow, and then a torrent. Within weeks it was clear that we would more than break even.

We began getting lots of free publicity, not just from college newspapers, but from local newspapers, radio, and TV. Whenever possible, we directed them to our panel of contest judges. In just a few months, Ira's plan had become a reality. And very soon, we would learn who had written The Great American Term Paper.

5

The announcement of the name of the contest winner was a major media event. Each of the four national TV networks sent a camera crew to the campus of the tiny Midwest liberal arts college that she attended. Offers flooded in for full scholarships from dozens of journalism schools, as well as job offers from major newspapers and magazines to each of the five prize winners and to many of the students who had received honorable mention.

In the meantime, I had quite unexpectedly been promoted to full professor, and was becoming something of a celebrity in academic circles. Best of all, I would no longer need to teach summer classes.

But something had been bothering me. I needed to have a serious talk with Ira. He had alluded to a long-term plan for making a lot more money. The Great American Term Paper Contest would be just a stepping-stone.

So, one evening we met at our favorite hangout, *The Majestic Diner* on Kings Highway, two blocks off Ocean Parkway. Ira was ready to lay out his master plan.

"First of all, you understand that e-mail lists can be very valuable—especially lists of college students."

I nodded. *That* I could live with.

But Ira had a still better idea.

Rather than sell the lists, we could rent them out—over and over again. We could limit each customer to just a single use of the list, so he can't steal it from us.

I smiled. My old friend thought of everything.

"Moving right along," he said, "let's get to the tricky part."

I gave him a sharp look.

"Yes, Dan. This is the part that you may not like. In fact, I would be surprised if you did."

Now he *really* had my attention.

"Ira, we've been friends for a long time. I know you like to take chances sometimes. Big risks, really. So, tell me right up front, is this thing you have in mind…"

"Legal?"

"Yeah, is it legal?"

"To be absolutely truthful, I don't know. It's kind of in a gray area."

"OK, then let me rephrase: Is it moral?"

"That depends on who's answering. To me, it's just business."

"And to me?"

"Well, we all have to decide for ourselves. But I strongly suspect that you would find this *quite* immoral."

"Ira, I love you like a brother. But I think for both our sakes, we better end this discussion right now."

"Fine. So, here's the deal: I will not involve you in any way with what I'm going to do. It will be completely separate from

The Great American Term Paper Contest. In fact, what we can do in the next few days is talk to a lawyer. Or maybe have *your* lawyer and *my* lawyer talk to each other."

"Ira, I appreciate your honesty—*and* about your looking out for my best interests. But I'm still worried about *you*. Are you sure you know what you're getting yourself into?"

"Right now, let's just worry about *you*. Like you said, I'm a risk-taker. And you'll agree, it's hard to win big unless you take big risks."

6

Two weeks later, Ira and I signed the papers. He bought out my half of the business. He would continue to run the contest, and I would go back to being a full time academic. In fact, the word on the street was that the City University would soon make me a distinguished professor. You might say that, without having written a word, *I* was the biggest winner of The Great American Term Paper contest.

I had no idea what Ira was up to, and I really didn't *want* to know. Soon we began to drift apart, and I wondered if perhaps he was distancing himself to protect me.

When my daughter graduated from high school, he wrote her a huge check. It worried me, but I just thanked him for his generosity. A year later, when Ira came to my son's bar mitzvah, I kidded him about how much Larry had earned for each word of his Torah portion.

When we did talk, neither of us ever mentioned Ira's business activities. He had joined a few charity boards and was often mentioned in the newspapers—even on page six of "The Jewish Daily Post." I just hoped he would be alright—*whatever* it was that he was doing.

7

A month later, completely out of the blue, he called to give me some utterly unexpected news. "Dan, you're not going to believe this! I'm making *Aliyah!*"

49

"What? You're moving to Israel? Permanently? Are you nuts?"

"I suppose I am. Anyway, I'm at Kennedy right now. My flight leaves in an hour."

"Will I ever *see* you again?"

"Of *course*! Look, I gotta go now. I'll call you in a couple of days."

When he hung up, I was left trying to digest what he had said. Was he in trouble? Was the FBI or the NYPD breathing down his neck? Did this have anything to do with his business?

Two days later, it was all over the news, along with his photo. The Great American Term Paper Contest had been just a front for Ira's *real* business. And the currency used by *that* business was the hundreds of thousands of term papers that had been submitted to the contest each year.

These papers had been sold at the bargain rate of a dollar a page to term paper mills, which then resold them for ten, or even twenty dollars a page to lazy students. In his defense, it could be said that not *one* of the papers he sold was a prize-winner, or even an honorable mention. Right, I thought: A thief with honor.

It took a while for all of this to sink in. Ira was safe in Israel, and he had done everything possible to protect me. That included providing what lawyers call "plausible deniability." I truly had no idea what he had been up to. Still, that was because I didn't *want* to know. When the Chancellor of the City University asked if I had known what Ira would do, I told her about our conversation at the Mirage Diner. So yes, I had some premonition that he might be up to no good; but no, I did not have a clue as to *what* he might actually do. She said that it certainly appeared that Ira had wanted to protect me, and that he had succeeded

Was this the end of The Great American Term Paper Contest? If anything, the scandal seemed to have had the opposite effect. A new group of contest judges—all truly distinguished professors representing the nation's most prestigious colleges and universities—provided at least a patina of impeccable rectitude.

The contest was bigger than ever, with students from nearly every college competing. The prize money was quintupled, and there were now one thousand honorable mentions. Offers of scholarships and jobs multiplied. And perhaps most importantly, a valuable lesson had been learned. Like our huge banks, The Great American Term Paper Contest was too big to fail.

Magazine Madness

It seemed a mistake when I received a copy of *Modern Bride*, since I'm not planning to get married, and also because I'm a guy. But there was my name on the mailing label. The next day, when *Good Housekeeping* and *Woman's Day* arrived, I knew that something funny was going on. It had to be Arnie, my closest friend! Although now in our thirties, we still live at home, and have been playing practical jokes on each other since the second grade.

A day later, the postman rang the bell—not twice—but *six* times. He handed me copies of *Vogue, Woman's World, Redbook, Glamour, Elle,* and *Seventeen*. We just stood there, silently eying each other. Then, in a very plaintive tone, he asked, "Who *does* this?"

Later that day, when Arnie and I got together, I asked him what was up with the magazines. At first, he played innocent. But when he could contain himself no longer, he gleefully admitted that he had been sending magazines to a few select friends and family members.

"You are a very sick person, Arnie. But you already know that. So permit me ask: *Why* are you doing this?"

"Because I *can!*"

"That's a cop-out if I ever heard one!"

"Because it's fun?"

"*Now* you're talking!"

But then I realized his subscription plan did have one serious drawback. "Arnie, isn't this costing the magazine publishers a bundle for printing and postage?"

"Sure. But they can more than make up for that by charging higher advertising rates."

"I don't think I follow."

"The more magazines they sell, the more they can raise their advertising rates."

"But they're not *selling* these magazines. No one is paying for them."

"True, but as long as the magazine publishers don't tell their advertisers, these subscriptions will *count* as paid."

"Are you sure about this?"

"I am, Bob. You know those discounts that are offered to college students?

"Would you believe I got an offer in the mail the other day? The headline was something like, "Deep discounts: up to 85 percent off many magazines."

"Shit! That's almost as good as the deal I give *my* quote unquote subscribers."

"So it doesn't matter whether people pay full price, half price, or none of the price: They're still counted as paid subscribers?"

"Correct. And as long as they're paid subscriptions, the advertisers don't care."

Still, there was something about Arnie's scheme that wasn't adding up. "You're telling me that when I got *Modern Bride*, someone actually paid for it?"

"Well technically, *you* did."

"How?"

"The card that I filled out for you had a box which I checked off. It said, 'Bill me later.'"

"I don't believe this!"

"So, in a couple of months, you'll get a bill, and then, a second notice, and maybe even a third notice. But don't worry: If you don't pay, they probably won't cut you off for another few months. And in the meanwhile, you'll be carried on their books as a paid subscriber."

"You're actually serious?"

"Look at it this way: Everybody wins. Subscriptions go up, sales of the advertised products go up, magazine advertising rates go up, and you get to read *Modern Bride* for free."

"And you want *me* to participate in this fraudulent undertaking?"

"Exactly!"

"When do we start?"

We spent the rest of the day at the neighborhood library pulling post card ordering forms from hundreds of magazines. And then we went back to my house and began sorting them.

My parents never asked what we were doing, and we never told.

One of our favorite ploys was sending a gift subscription of *New York Magazine* to a friend, and the bill to someone he or she knows. So Mel sends it to Sue and gets the bill. Then we reverse the process and have Sue donate a subscription to Mel. Repeating this process dozens of times, we solidified many friendships, while expanding cultural horizons.

Next, we started messing with people's heads by signing them up for magazines they probably hated. We sent gay magazines to straight guys, retirement magazines to teenagers, and sex magazines to fundamentalist Christians, Orthodox Jews, and deeply devout Muslims. Did we *miss* anybody?

Then, we wanted to see how subscription departments would handle unusual names. Their employees sometimes assumed the names had been misspelled. And so, Hitlerella Olson was changed to Hilterella Olson. Come on now, did you ever meet someone name Hilterella? Colonel Bloodstock-Shit became Colonel Bloodstock-Smith. But M. Cowflop Putzhead actually went through unchanged. As did Jesus Mohamed Schwartz, Colon Oscopy UpJohn, Mao Tse O'Connor, and T. Thomas Thimblecock.

One day I got an urgent phone call from Arnie. "You've got to get over here right away! There's been a new development."

When I got there, instead of inviting me in, he said we needed to go for a walk.

"Arnie, are we in trouble?"

"No, I don't want my parents to hear this conversation."

"What happened?"

"I got a call today from a lawyer. She represents one of the big magazines we've been ripping off."

"Are they suing us?"

"No, just the opposite! She said that they had finally figured out what we were up to, and that their advertising revenues were up twenty percent in the last quarter. So the publisher wants to arrange discrete quarterly payments that would be kept strictly confidential."

"I can't believe this! How much will we get?"

"Bob, would you believe they're giving us ten thousand dollars every three months?"

"That's amazing!"

"There's more! She has agreed to represent three other magazines which would also like to send us payments."

"And there's no catch?"

"Just that if we keep doing what we're doing, they'll keep paying us."

"You know, with this deal, we can still live with our parents while we're paid to have fun."

"That's right, Bob. We never have to grow up."

The Rip-Off Artist

I know a young Chinese man named Fong. He grew up not far from Hong Kong and came here when he was in his early twenties. He had studied painting for years, learning to imitate the work of the old masters.

He arrived penniless, with virtually nothing but a few dozen of his paintings and the clothes on his back. He quickly found a job washing dishes in New York's Chinatown, and a bed to sleep on in a cramped apartment that was fully occupied by recent immigrants sleeping in shifts.

Slowly, Fong learned some English, and then met a beautiful young Chinese woman who had grown up just a few miles from him. He and Mudan soon found their own tiny apartment in a part of Little Italy where more people spoke Chinese rather than Italian or English.

Fong was able to resume painting. Their friends admired his work, but none could pay more than a few dollars for one of his beautiful watercolors. Surely, in such a rich country, there were people who could afford his work.

By now, the Soho art scene was going full blast, and customers were spending tens and even hundreds of thousands of dollars on paintings by hot young artists with no apparent talent. But most of them did manage to be born into rich families that sent them to fancy art schools, supported them with generous trust funds, and sent their friends and business associates to buy their children's work.

One day, Mudan told him about her business idea. They would go into business together selling his paintings. Fong listened patiently, but deep down he knew it would never work.

Still, it wouldn't hurt to humor her. Every evening after work, they would rehearse. If nothing else, they would have a skit that might amuse their friends.

After two weeks, Mudan said that they were ready. They would go to Chinatown where there were several stores that sold watercolors painted by old Chinese masters hundreds of years ago. Most of the customers were very rich Chinese tourists as well as first- and second-generation Chinese Americans.

Few of them appeared to know much about these ancient Chinese masters, but virtually all believe they knew good art when they saw it. If you buy what you like, how can you go wrong? And besides, over time, the value of these paintings could only go up.

Mudan had fully coached him on his pitch. But he was very nervous about their new business enterprise, so she decided to put that nervousness to good advantage.

They walked down to Chinatown the next morning. They had a list of stores that had ancient Chinese watercolors for sale along with more recent paintings. When they entered the first store on their list, the shop owner barely glanced at them. He was on the phone, apparently in the middle of a heated argument.

Finally, when the man got off the phone, Fong approached him and asked very politely in Chinese if he might be interested in buying an ancient Chinese watercolor. The owner looked at him with suspicion. How indeed could this poor guy, probably just off the boat, possibly come to own such a painting?

Then, Mudan joined them, asking in English, "Please, sir, could you just *look* at it? It belonged to his grandfather."

Fong kept his eyes downcast as he unwrapped the painting. The owner glanced at it, and then quickly did a double take. How could this country bumpkin possibly have come into possession of such a masterpiece?

It was almost definitely not a counterfeit. After more than twenty years in the business, he was pretty certain he had been tricked no more than two or three times. And even *then*, he was able to find gullible buyers.

If this one was authentic, he might even be willing to offer as much as five or ten percent of what he estimated it was worth. He was sure it would fetch at least ten or fifteen thousand, even if he was not one hundred percent certain of its authenticity.

But then he began to grow suspicious, since Fong was clearly very nervous.

"OK, how much are you asking for this painting?"

Fong glanced at his girlfriend, who nodded.

"Please make me a fair offer. I will accept an offer that is fair."

The owner thought this over. Clearly, this peasant had no idea how much his painting was worth. So, he reached into his pocket, pulled out a wad of bills, and started counting them out, "Twenty, forty, sixty, eighty, one hundred... one hundred-twenty ... one-hundred-forty...

Suddenly, Fong picked up the painting and began wrapping it.

The owner was taken aback. "Perhaps there is a misunderstanding."

"There is no misunderstanding," replied Fong. "You are trying to cheat me. *That* is not hard to understand!"

"OK, let me have another look at your painting."

Fong glanced at Mudan. She shrugged.

Fong hesitated, and then very slowly unwrapped the painting and placed it back on the counter.

The owner examined it more closely. While there was no way he could identify the painter, he recognized the centuries-old style. He felt the rice paper with his fingertips, and pretty much knew for sure it was definitely the real thing.

But where could this poor soul have possibly obtained this painting? Did he steal it? Did he somehow acquire it from a friend who knew even less about ancient Chinese art?

The owner now began to realize that perhaps this young man actually *did* have some idea of how much this painting might be worth. Counting out those bills was very stupid of him. Insulting the young man was probably going to cost him.

But before he could offer more for the painting, he had to be absolutely one-hundred percent certain that it was not just a cleverly executed imitation.

He put on what appeared to be a pair of very thick reading glasses. Fong knew he was examining the brush strokes—the ultimate test of authenticity.

Then he removed the glasses and very slowly, almost imperceptibly, he began to shake his head as if he were disagreeing with someone—possibly even himself. He was frowning.

Fong sensed that the man was displeased. But when he glanced at Mudan, she was smiling. She had seen the man clenching and unclenching his fists. Clearly, he was attempting to stifle his emotion.

The owner quickly did a final estimate in his head. He could easily sell this for at least twenty thousand dollars—and possibly much more. Should he make an offer? Or should he ask the young man how much he wanted?

If he offered too little, the young man would probably be infuriated and leave with his painting. But if he offered what was truly a fair price, then that would greatly reduce his customary profit.

Then, he had a much *better* idea. Trying to sound as casual as possible, the owner asked, "How much do *you* think would be a fair price for this painting?"

Fong and his girlfriend immediately stepped several feet away and went into a huddle. They whispered back and forth for a couple of minutes. Finally, Fong approached the counter.

"We want four thousand dollar." He folded his arms across his chest, trying to look determined.

"Three *thousand!*" the owner countered.

"Three thousand, five hundred and not a penny less!" said the girlfriend.

"In cash!" added Fong

The owner knew he had just seconds to make a decision.

"It's a *deal!*"

The next morning, a nervous-looking young man and a beautiful young woman entered a small shop in Brooklyn's rapidly expanding Chinatown. They glanced around, and then approached the counter.

The Basketball Hustler

Many of the great basketball players have had rhyming nicknames like Wilt the Stilt, Earl the Pearl, or Dean the Dream. Although even I would never compare myself with those immortals, as a teenager I was known by the alliterative—if not rhyming—appellation of Steve the Shot.

The only problem was that in a game of big men sprinting down the court and then pulling up for deadly jump shots, I was the last high school basketball player to live and die by shooting fifteen and twenty-foot set shots. For those of you too young to have even heard of this shot, it's quite simple. You stand there holding the ball chest-high, draw a bead on the basket, and *swish!*

For me, set shots were almost as easy as shooting foul shots. I would hit three-quarters of my shots, even with an opponent waving his hands three inches from my face. If you look up the records of all the New York City high school players from my era, not one of them came even close to my record for accuracy.

But our high school coach—once an All-American college basketball player—would tell me that not only had the game passed me by, but that the set shot was obsolete years before I was born. The man clearly knew what he was talking about since he had taken our team to the finals of the city championship more often than any other coach in New York.

He did keep me on the team, but about the only chance I got to play was during what's known as "garbage time," when we were playing in a blowout. "Steve," he would say, "You're too short and you're too slow, so even if you're the greatest shooter in the world, you're never going to make it in this game."

I suppose I should have been grateful that he kept me on the team, but he warned me that no college team would want me. I wanted to prove him wrong, but the only team that showed any interest was a tiny school in Ohio that had fewer than 200 students. They couldn't give me a scholarship, but they managed to cobble together a package of student aid, some loans and a promise to be a starter for my entire college career. It was an offer I could not afford to refuse.

Believe it or not, I quickly began getting tons of press coverage because of my prolific scoring. I took half our shots and made three-quarters of them.

Newspaper reporters and even TV guys came from all over the country to cover my anachronistic shooting skills. When I scored sixty-three points against Sitting Bull College—and if you don't believe there *is* such a school, go ahead and google it—our team became *America's* team—even if such a team played only against such rivals as *Slippery Rock, Stanley Kaplan University,* and the *Bible College of the Ozarks.*

But as we know, all good things come to an end. After a four-year career in which I set seasonal and career scoring records for players at the nation's unranked colleges, I finally graduated. And all I had to show for it was a stack of newspaper clippings and tens of thousands of dollars in student debt.

When I came home to Brooklyn, just a few of my friends were still around, and no one even called me "Steve the Shot" anymore. My career was over and I needed to get serious about not just paying off my student loans, but thinking about what I wanted to do for the rest of my life.

My parents were glad to have me at home again, but I knew that they were too polite to even ask what my plans were. And if they had, I don't know what I could have told them.

To stay in some kind of shape, I decided to join one of those rag-tag teams of former high school ballplayers that essentially played for beer money. But I got the shock of my life. None of them wanted me. I was tempted to come back with all my clippings and throw them in their faces, but what would *that* get me?

I don't know if it was worry or simple genetics, but my hair started going gray. In an effort to keep my youthful appearance, I shaved my head. Then I realized doing so made me look still older. One of the black guys I had played with in high school kidded me that my new hairstyle worked only for black guys who were going bald.

"You just joined the wrong race, Shot."

Then, one day, it suddenly hit me: I knew immediately that I had not only found a way to make a good living, but that I would also extract some measure of revenge for how I had been treated—not to mention how unjustly my talents had been overlooked.

Brooklyn has dozens of playgrounds and in most of them there are plenty of teenagers who are so confident of their talents, they are always looking to play basketball for money. They'd play one-on-one, two against two, and sometimes three-man basketball.

I liked one-on-one because there was virtually no way I could lose. In the customary game the first to get ten baskets was the winner. And the guy who scores last takes out the ball. So, if one guy got very hot, he might win ten-zip, ten-one or ten-two.

Usually, we'd play for a couple of dollars, but I had heard there were games where the stakes were considerably higher. Some guys could walk away with close to a thousand bucks.

I knew that I had two big things going for me. My great set shot and how my opponents perceived me. Remember the old saying from the sixties—don't trust anyone over thirty? Well, let's put it *this* way: No one trusted my basketball talents—not to mention their suspicions that I was probably pushing thirty.

I decided to start small. I'd play teenaged kids for just a buck or two a game. I quickly realized that I needed to brush up on my defensive skills. Some of the taller guys would bully their way to the basket. I quickly figured out how to distract them by constantly calling offensive fouls.

In playground basketball you call a foul by yelling, "I got it!" All that means is that play is stopped for a few seconds. Then it resumes pretty much where you left off. But I found that I could upset the rhythm of my opponent and also make him think twice about bullying his way to the basket for an easy layup.

Still, my main weapon remained my set shot. No one could believe my accuracy. They'd just stand there, several feet away from me, daring me to shoot. And I did, again, and again, and again.

It's pretty hard to beat a guy who could routinely hit more than three-quarters of his shots from around the circle. Especially such an old, out-of-shape guy.

I knew that I couldn't keep playing in the same four or five playgrounds every day since it wouldn't take long for the kids to catch on to me. And besides, most of them couldn't afford to bet more than a few bucks on a game. But luckily, I had discovered the private school crowd—essentially a bunch of spoiled, rich white boys.

These fellas almost all had highly inflated opinions of their basketball talents. Still, had I been a tall black guy with flashy moves, they would never have taken me on.

By now I had developed an effective financial strategy. I'd flash a wad of bills before the first game. And I'd make sure— win or lose—that the first game was pretty close. Then, I'd offer to double the stakes. After just four or five games, I'd walk away with six or eight hundred bucks.

These private school kids loved playing two-on-two. As they caught on that I was a deadly set shot shooter, my teammate would gladly keep feeding me the ball.

I became friendly with a few of them. We'd hustle games together with other groups of private school boys. Soon I could count on a steady income of over a thousand dollars a day.

I decided to let my hair grow in. At the same time, I stopped shaving. Just as I suspected, when my beard started growing in, it was white. One morning, when I looked in the mirror I saw an old friend I had once read about. His name was Rip Van Winkle.

My new appearance really helped my image and boosted my earnings. Who could resist taking money from this crazy old man? On some really good days, I was winning as much as two thousand dollars.

Then I made a very smart business decision. Since I no longer needed the money, I would preserve my career by carefully picking my games and my playing partners. By playing just on weekends, I could extend my career. Indeed, I found myself playing for the fun of it even more than for the money.

Who would have thought that my playing days would last much longer than those of my old high school teammates, several of whom actually went on to careers in the NBA and still others who played in the European professional basketball leagues? And what would my old coach have thought?

But time passes quickly when you're having fun. In my case, that time was measured over decades. One day I woke up and realized that I would soon hit the big five-oh. I wasn't sure how much longer I could keep playing.

I had already made some adjustments. I scaled down my bets and was once again playing for just a few dollars a game. I was even losing a bit of my competitive edge. And I began to think seriously about a life after basketball.

One day, after I mopped the floor with a couple of teenage kids, we sat around chewing the fat. Reggie said he'd like to ask me a personal question "if that would be OK."

"Sure, you can ask me anything."

He looked at his friend, Chas, and then he asked me how I had managed to keep in such great shape.

"Well," I replied, "I do three things every night."

I saw that I had their attention. I guess they really wanted to know my secret. Maybe, when they were as old as I was, they could be just like me.

"I know I may not look to you like someone who indulges, but I *do* like to have an occasional drink."

"What do you drink?" asked Reggie.

"I happen to like vodka. I drink a fifth of it every night."

"Seriously?"

"Of course, Reggie!"

"Wow! So, what's the second thing you do?" asked Chas.

"I don't get much sleep. I'm lucky to get more than two or three hours."

"That's amazing!"

"Amazing, but true."

"And the third thing you do every night?" asked Reggie.

"I sleep with a woman—and sometimes *more* than one woman."

The two of them just shook their heads. Was this old guy just putting them on, or was he actually being straight with them?

Finally, Reggie wanted to know if it would be OK to ask just one more personal question.

"Of course."

"Do you mind my asking how *old* you are?"

"Of course not!"

I watched their faces, letting them wait for my answer. Then, after clearing my throat, I looked them straight in the eye.

"Just a few weeks ago I turned twenty-three."

Frankie's Last Con

Frankie and I go way back. We've known each other since the third grade and have managed to have kept up for all these years. So, I may be perhaps the most qualified of all his friends and acquaintances to describe him in just two words—con artist.

What does that say about *me?* Perhaps I can argue that despite this awful character flaw, Frankie is actually a pretty nice guy. He's fun to be around and he has a great imagination. And besides, nobody's perfect!

In fact, it was back in the third grade when he began working what would become his most enduring con. "Hey Steve, can I borrow a quarter? I'll pay you back tomorrow."

I caught on very quickly that tomorrow would never come. When this stopped working with me, he would try the same trick with other kids. In fact, a bunch of us used to say to each other, "For Frankie, give no quart" even if not all of us fully understood the second definition of "quarter."

In high school, a bunch of us would chip in to pay for parties. Frankie would always offer to pay later. You know how *that* worked out.

Maybe, if he came from a poor family, that might explain his behavior. But his dad was a bigshot lawyer, and sometimes even got his name in the newspaper. I remember how he even defended some guy in the Mafia.

So, Frankie was definitely not hurting for money. In fact, he was the first person I knew whose parents bought him a car. It goes without saying that every time he offered one of us a ride, he would ask for gas money.

So why was Frankie always pulling these cons—especially since he clearly did not need the money? Yvonne, who was majoring in psychology at Barnard said that he was just doing it because he *could.* Even if you have plenty of money, she added, you ask yourself, "Why pay, when I can get it for free?"

So, for Frankie, there was great joy in pulling the strings of friends and strangers as well. The thrill was in getting away with something, rather than even enjoying your ill-gotten gains.

I recall a news story about a noted pickpocket who was caught red-handed with his hand in another man's back pocket. He readily admitted to the arresting police officer that he had already taken the wallet just to see if he could, and that he had been caught putting it back.

I wondered if that was what drove Frankie—just seeing what he could get away with. Maybe he had no control over his impulses. But I also wondered why I remained friends with him.

One day he came to me with an offer that I could not refuse. If I lent him a thousand dollars, he would pay me back one thousand five hundred dollars in just three months.

I thanked him, but politely refused his offer. Not long after that, he disappeared. No one saw him around the neighborhood, and his phone was disconnected.

Two years later I got a call from him. He had changed his name, moved out of the city, and he wanted to know if anyone was still looking for him. I told him that people who get screwed like that have long memories.

"Look Steve, *you* I woulda paid back."

"With interest?"

"Well, maybe not with interest."

The next time we saw each other was the day after the 25th reunion of our high school graduation. One of our classmates held a huge party in her home and charged everyone just five dollars apiece.

Frankie showed up with his wife, who had graduated a few years after we did. I saw them standing in the doorway, talking to the hostess. Sure enough, he was asking if they could come in for just a couple of minutes.

She turned them down and they left. She saw me looking at her and we both started laughing. "Does a leopard change his stipes?" she asked.

He was lucky no one he had conned into lending him a thousand dollars all those years ago had spotted him. The cost of his admission would have been a lot more than five dollars.

At least twenty more years had gone by when I heard that his wife had died. I had intended to send my condolences, but I had no way of reaching him.

But then, just the other day, he e-mailed me. This would be Frankie's last con.

Hello, I hope you are doing well. Wishing you a Happy New Month with Covid free.

Stay safe

Thanks Frankie! You too!

I am so sorry to hear about your wife.

Best regards,

Steve

Thanks Steve,

I'm sorry to bother you with these. But I really do need help picking up a (GOOGLE GIFT CARD) for my niece.

She's a year older today. I tried to purchase one online using my Giftcard.com account. Unfortunately, it was declined several times for some reason I don't know why. My limit is $2,000 and I still should be able to charge about $1,500. If you could put down just $250—either cash or on a major credit card—I can reimburse you later this week.

Hi Frankie,

I have no idea what giftcard.com or a Google gift card, for that matter. Good luck with that!

Steve

Hi Steve

It's sad I can't take care of it at the moment... I'd just lost a childhood friend (Stacey). She died of the world's most deadly disease (Covid-19); her funeral is held at noon today.

Would you be kind enough to pick it up for me anytime you can today?

Sorry for the inconvenience.

The Broadway Actors Matrimonial Service

My name is Sergei and I managed to get out of Romania almost thirty years ago by paying an American woman $10,000 to marry me. We got married at City Hall, just a few hundred feet from the Brooklyn Bridge, and I never saw her again.

I got a job working for my boyhood friend, Serene, who also came here by marrying an American. But they actually loved each other and remain married to this day.

Serene had always liked the theater, and he hired me to assist him. He was what is called a *house paperer*. Every day he bought up several hundred theater tickets for off-Broadway plays—usually for just two or three dollars apiece—and resold them for eight or ten dollars.

Everybody came out ahead. The ticket buyers got deeply discounted seats without having to wait on long lines and picked up their tickets within blocks of the theater. The actors play to full houses. And Serene made money. So what was *not* to like?

Serene had three other Romanians working for him, none of whom had a green card, which would have entitled them to work here legally. Virtually all of the ticket buyers were regulars, and everything was on the up-and-up.

But after a couple of years, I began to grow restless. So I decided to move on. I did a little of this and a little of that, while I always had my house papering gig to fall back on.

It wasn't until about twenty-five years later that my luck suddenly changed. My friend Caroline asked me for "a great big favor."

"How big?"

"Well, Sergei, I'll let *you* be the judge of that."

Caroline, who is a fairly prominent author, had not been to her office in over two weeks. Why? Someone had been murdered in the building.

Like me, Caroline is nocturnal, never getting up before two or three in the afternoon. Luckily, her office is in a building that stays open 24/7. But on the downside, it is largely unoccupied after 8 or 9 pm.

"So would you be able to stay with me for five or six hours, while I go through all my mail, and try to get a little work done?"

"Sure. But why don't you just take all the mail home?"

"Three reasons. First, it's too much to bring home. I'd rather have a messy office than a messy apartment. Second, I'd then have to lug some of it back to the office. And third, the main reason I rent the office is to go through the mail and store my files."

I love Caroline, and one of her charms is that she can be a little compulsive. In fact, she's written three books on organizing your life, and she had won some kind of award from a group that advocates for people with psychological disorders similar to her own.

So there was no way I could argue against her logic. "Of course Caroline. I would be most happy to help you."

"Great! Maybe bring along a book to read. I promise it won't be more than six hours."

At 8pm the next evening, we met in front of an old seven-storey building on Third Ave. just below 14th Street. A uniformed guard asked for our IDs and had us sign in. Then he went back to whatever he was watching on a small TV and we took the elevator to the top floor. We walked down a long corridor lined with doors with frosted windows.

As we walked, I asked, "Are these all offices?"

"I think so. If they came in dress sizes, mine would be a 1. In fact, my office is actually divided into two cubicles."

"Who has the other one?"

"Sergei, did you ever hear of Elaine Champagne?"

"I'm afraid not. I just got off the boat."

"You got off the boat twenty-five years ago, Anyway, Elaine was a very highly regarded theatrical agent."

"What happened to her? No wait! Let me guess, she drank too much of the bubbly stuff and lost all of her clients."

"Worse! *Much* worse! Her son, who was in his mid-twenties, and a newlywed, committed suicide."

I just stared at Caroline.

"She hasn't been back to her office since then. Not even to pick up her mail. And for all I know, maybe all of her clients *did* leave her."

"That is such an awful story. You're not in touch with her?"

"I've tried calling her and leaving messages. But it's been two years. The only thing I know is that she still pays the rent on her office."

We stopped at a door near the end of the hall, and she let us in. It was a windowless room divided into two cubicles, each about ten by twelve feet.

Caroline immediately got down to work, and I squeezed into Elaine Champagne's cubicle. It was almost entirely filled with stacks of mail. Imagine if you went to the main post office when they were on strike.

I cleared off her chair and a little space on her desk. But I had to be careful not to cause an avalanche. There had to be tens of thousands of pieces of mail. I began going through a small stack. On top was a postcard with a glossy headshot of a smiling guy who reminded me of the actor Ashton Kutcher. On the back was a note about a showcase he was staring in. Next was a card from a beautiful woman who proudly noted her appearance in a Volvo commercial.

I went through another dozen cards before it struck me that nobody had a clue that Elaine Champagne was no longer in the industry. They were doing mass mailings to every New York theatrical agent in the hopes that one would take them on. How sad is *that*?

I kept reading. A lot of the notes struck a personal tone, as if Ms. Champagne closely followed the actors' careers: "In case you missed me on the HBO special, it will be rebroadcast next Sunday at 4pm." Or, "Please keep me in mind for a role, however small, in any upcoming musicals."

Finally, we were ready for a break. Caroline explained that hundreds of these cards still arrived every week. Everybody needed a theatrical agent—even one who might be terminally depressed. When I went back to the mail, I decided to put all the headshot cards into two neat piles—boys in one pile and girls in the other. I'm not *that* much of a neatnik, but an idea was beginning to form, and I knew that I would find a use for them.

When we were getting ready to leave, I asked Caroline if I could take some of the cards home.

"Sure! Take *all* of them! God only knows if Elaine will ever be back!"

So I filled a couple of shopping bags, and we made our way down to the street. I walked her home and then spent the rest of the night figuring out what I would do with the cards. Early the next afternoon when I woke up, I grabbed a piece of paper and wrote down these words: The Broadway Actors Matrimonial Service. It turned out to be the best idea I had ever had.

Remember the $10,000 I paid an American woman to marry me? What we formed had long been known as a "green card marriage," because an immigrant who marries an American can get an expedited green card, or work permit. There are hundreds of thousands of Eastern European men and women who would agree to pay someone a lot more than $10,000 to go through with this charade.

So far, so good. Foreigners are willing to pay their way into the United States, and there are Americans willing to be paid to marry them. So why not arrange marriages between Eastern Europeans and American actors and actresses?

Tens of thousands of actors live in New York, but only a very small percentage of them can support themselves by acting—*or* doing commercials. Most of them get by with relatively low-paying jobs like waiting tables, tending bar, doing office temp work, and providing childcare. Many of them were saddled with huge student debts. I was sure that some would jump at the chance to pick up a sizeable amount of money by agreeing to a green card marriage.

But wait, there's more! What if we could add a sweetener? Even more than money, what most actors crave is finding a theatrical agent. Let me add here that we're not talking about just some schmuck who claims to be an agent, but can't do anything for his clients that they can't do on their own. No, I mean a real, honest-to-goodness, seasoned, respected, and *legitimate* theatrical agent.

I talked this over with Serene. He had an idea. There were three agents who shared an office on Broadway in the forties. They had a perfect location. There was only one problem. Their landlord wanted to double their rent. There was no way they could manage it. And there wasn't any other suitable space they could afford in the theatrical district.

Serene made the connection. "If we set up a bunch of green card marriages of actors and Eastern Europeans—and take a cut of the dowry—we could keep these agents in business."

"Wow!" I immediately saw the light. "And then we could offer their services to the new brides and grooms as a kind of wedding present." Leave it to two Romanian immigrants to make the American dream come true.

In a few weeks a couple of our old friends in Romania had created a website on which were headshots of dozens of very attractive actors and actresses. Are you wondering why we bothered setting up in Romania? Well, think about it! If you saw *your* picture on someone's website—and they were using it to make money, wouldn't *you* demand that they stop?

But if that website happened to be in a country like Romania or Moldavia or Russia—it would be much less likely that they would comply. And it might be almost impossible to sue.

Another potential problem would also be averted. While green card marriages are legal, the State Department would find ways to shut us down if we operated in the U.S.

On Valentine's Day of 2011, a few dozen actors and actresses received the following email:

> We are an international talent agency based in Eastern Europe, and would like to make you an interesting two-part offer. First, if you are willing to enter into a "green card" marriage with someone from Eastern Europe, you will be paid $35,000. Your spouse needs to be legally married in order to live in the United States, and to obtain a green card.

Before you take your vows, each of you will have in hand a "no-fault" divorce agreement. Once you are married, you will be under no obligation to ever see each other ever again. Your only obligation will be to stay married until your spouse receives her or his green card. Now comes even better news. We can get you representation with a reputable theatrical agent based in the theater district.

Within hours after our email went out, we began receiving replies. Some were a little nasty: "How DARE you invade my privacy!" "DIE!!!" "Rot in Hell!"

Others were somewhat quizzical: "Is this a joke?" "Are you legit?" "How did you get my email address?"

But a few actually asked how they could sign up.

In the meanwhile, we spread the word through social media and some carefully placed ads throughout the former Soviet bloc nations for green card seekers. We were completely upfront that it would cost them $50,000.

The response was unbelievable! Serene and I joked that we should become ordained ministers and perform mass marriages at Yankee Stadium. Our Romanian counterparts addressed us as the Rev Serene and the Rev Sergei. That made us feel like real Americans.

On June 3rd Serene and I witnessed the first marriage, which was held at City Hall. And before the summer was over, there were twenty-three more. We were on our way.

Just before Christmas, a new bride, who had signed with one of our agents got a part in a Broadway play. To celebrate, Serene and I had dinner at Sardi's.

"So what's our next move?"

"I don't know, Sergei. You're the idea man."

"Thanks, Serene. You wanna know what I was thinking?"

"Sure."

"Well, with all our contacts and the money we've been making, why don't we produce our own play?"

"OK, I'm listening."

"I've already got the title. We'll call it, 'The Broadway Actors Matrimonial Service.'"

"So far, so good."

"We already have the cast."

"We *do*?"

"Sure Serene. Our newlyweds."

"That's going to be a pretty large cast."

"If we were making a movie, most of them would be extras. Well actually, we can give them relative short speaking parts."

Serene sat there letting this all sink in. Then I continued.

"Now hold on to your seat. Our play is going to be on Broadway."

"What are you nuts, Sergei? Who would put *our* play on Broadway?"

"We will!"

"Sergei, you are one crazy Romanian! We're talking about filling the house with at least 500 tushies. How can we possibly do that night-after-night?"

I didn't say anything. After maybe six or eight seconds Serene began to smile. Then we burst out laughing. We would paper our own house!

"One week, limited engagement. Eight performances, which comes to 'selling' 4,000 seats. If we give each performer a couple of free tickets for each performance, that would take care of almost half the seats. And who knows, maybe we'll even sell some tickets."

Three months later, we were ready for opening night. There were no preview performances. We knew we would lose a lot of money on our scheme, but we were not at all prepared for what happened next. Predictably the critics were brutal. If you think of what Bialystock and Bloom had counted on happening when they put on *Springtime for Hitler*, it turns out "The Broadway Actors Matrimonial Service" exceeded even *those* low expectations. "Complete Shit!" headlined one of the kinder reviews we received. And unlike Bialystock and Bloom's play, ours was not perceived by audiences as a comedy. It was, by far, the *worst* play they had ever seen.

A reviewer for *The Times* suggested that if Tonys were given for "the worst" in all major categories, our play would make a clean sweep—except for the acting. As he pointed out, "Even the world's greatest acting ensemble could not have rescued this piece of *drek!*"

Alongside its review, *Variety* placed a cartoon with this caption: "What Hirschfeld would have drawn had he still been alive." Above the caption was a blank sheet of paper.

As word spread about the worst play in the history of Broadway, the completely unexpected happened. Legitimate ticket demand actually started climbing, and we were able to hold the play over for another week, and then still another. Audiences flocked to see for themselves just how *bad* a Broadway play could be. And they were not disappointed.

Our play finally closed after a very respectable six-month run. One week later an email blast went to over 2,000 actors and actresses:

We are an international talent agency based in Eastern Europe, and would like to extend a three-part offer. First, we will pay you $35,000 to temporarily marry someone from Eastern Europe who needs a green card. Second, we will provide representation with a highly successful American theatrical agent. And third, within the next year, you will be cast in a Broadway play.

Notes from Jeannie Kaplan

The promenade in Brooklyn Heights provides a great view of New York harbor. You can see the Statue of Liberty, the Brooklyn Bridge, the Staten Island Ferry, and, of course, the New York skyline. I was sitting on a bench with my legs stretched out and my face tilted up toward the sun. It was the first warm day of March, and I had just run back and forth a few times across the bridge. In the 1970s, it had not yet been discovered by tourists.

My eyes were closed, but I heard someone sit down near me.

"Did you go to Brooklyn College? I went there from 1958 to 1967. It took me that long because I changed majors six times. I graduated as a sociology major with minors in political science, history, and English."

Without bothering to open my eyes I muttered, "Maybe a little too much information."

She laughed. And that's what got me—the sound of it. It was sincere, self-deprecating, and pleasant.

I opened my eyes. She was fairly attractive, but what really caught my attention was her hair. It reminded me of Angela Davis's hair. In case you don't remember her, she was an extremely attractive black activist with a huge Afro. The woman sitting next to me had what would soon be termed a *Jewfro*.

"Jeannie Kaplan," she said as she extended her hand.

"Howie Greenberg. And yeah, I *did* go to Brooklyn."

"When did you graduate?"

"1957... No wait a minute, that's when I graduated from Madison. No, I graduated from Brooklyn in 1961."

"Yeah, so you *do* look familiar from college."

"I can't say that *you* do."

"No, probably not. I looked different then. Long straight hair—and I was always in the library studying. From the time I was in elementary school, if I came home with a 98, my mother asked me why I didn't get 99. And if I got a 99, she wanted to know why I didn't get 100."

"What if you got 100?"

"Then she'd find something else."

From what appeared to be a huge carpet bag, she pulled a pad of yellow legal size paper, wrote her phone number down, handed it to me, and then told me to write down my number. Glancing at her, I saw that she was perfectly serious, so I wrote my number.

Then she stood up and said, "I've got to run now. I'm already late for my therapist appointment. My parents pay for it, which makes me feel guilty, but then he and I have another thing to talk about."

I watched her as she rushed off down the promenade. She waved to a woman who waved back at her. Then she sat down again to begin another conversation.

I didn't call her and she didn't call me. Then, one weekday afternoon, I was running on the bridge and I saw her walking toward me. As we passed, I asked her to wait for me on the Brooklyn end of the bridge.

I reached the Manhattan side and ran back to Brooklyn. I passed a couple of dozen people walking home from work. As I approached the end of the bridge I didn't see Jeannie, but there was a smiling guy in a business suit. He was holding a yellow, legal size sheet of paper.

The note was almost a page long. It was an explanation of why she did not have the time to wait for me, but she definitely wanted to talk to me. Why did that not surprise me?

A week later I invited her to a party. I was having about ten friends over. She said she'd try to come if she didn't have too much work to do.

As the last couple was leaving, they handed me a note someone had pushed under my door. I laughed when I saw the yellow paper. Jeannie needed four pages to explain why she couldn't spare the time to attend my party. It probably took her over an hour to write the note.

I decided to invite her to dinner. We would meet at a restaurant on Montague Street the next evening.

When I got to the restaurant, she was already there. "I hate being late," she confided, "so I set my clocks and my watch half an hour early. I've actually been sitting here for thirty-seven minutes."

"So you must know what you'd like to order."

"Well, I was looking at the menu, but I couldn't decide whether to have a chef salad or a hamburger and fries."

"Didn't you have the same problem picking a major?"

"I told you, didn't I, that I had seven different majors at Brooklyn?"

"Yes, you certainly did."

The waitress approached and asked if we were ready to order. Jeannie had her face buried in the menu.

"Jeannie, why don't we start out with a plate of cold appetizers?" And we'll have more time to figure out what we want for entrees."

"OK, I sometimes have trouble making decisions."

The waitress, who was obviously used to this, said, "Plenty of time," and walked away. I asked Jeannie what she did for a living.

"I write term papers."

"I don't understand."

"I work for a term paper service. They pay me $1.50 a page."

"Isn't that illegal—not to mention unethical?"

"Well, to get around that, the company labels its service 'research.'"

"And you make a living doing this?'

"To be completely truthful, my parents help me. They pay my rent. Did I tell you that they also pay for my therapist?"

"Actually you did."

"I mean they *should*—after the way they screwed me up!"

It was hard for me to respond to that. If I agreed, that would imply that I thought she *was* screwed up. And if I didn't, then I was contradicting her. I just smiled.

"So how did you get into the term paper writing business?"

"It was easy. I knew someone who was working for the company. They actually advertise in *The Kingsman.*"

"Really? The college allows them to put ads in the student newspaper?"

"I think they have to. It's a first amendment issue—freedom of speech."

"Yeah, and freedom to cheat."

"Look, please don't *say* that! I feel guilty enough taking money to do this."

"So you're good at it?"

"Well, having gone through seven different majors, I'm pretty versatile."

The waitress returned with the appetizers. "Are you folks ready to order?"

I looked at Jeannie. Again, her face was buried in the menu. "Jeannie, why don't we share a chef's salad and a hamburger and French fries?"

"Sounds good to me!"

After the waitress left, I asked Jeannie if she had any long-term plans.

"I was hoping to go to grad school, but my father put his foot down. He said—and these were his exact words—'Young lady: with *your* academic track record, by the time you finish, you'll be an old lady!'"

"That's pretty harsh."

"Tell me about it!"

It turned out that Jeannie and I had a mutual friend. Harry was a research librarian at the Brooklyn Heights branch of the Brooklyn Public Library. One day, I saw her talking to him. When I walked over she began to introduce us, and then started laughing when she quickly realized that Harry and I already knew each other.

She proclaimed Harry "a great resource for term paper writing." But today was special. Jeannie had received a new assignment. She would be writing an entire Master's thesis. The pay was fantastic: $5 a page!

Harry and I just looked at each other. Obviously he felt the same way I did about her work. Later, after Jeannie went back to her cluttered table to go through the books Harry had given her, he confided how conflicted he felt about helping her.

"I try to rationalize by thinking that as a researcher, I need to be nonjudgmental. And that Jeannie is my friend. But on the other hand, I feel dirty. I'm complicit in facilitating this fraud. I've even consulted with my supervisor."

"Yeah?"

"She's as conflicted as *I* am. She said she would support me either way."

One day, Harry and I went for a long walk and ended up in front of the Grand Army Plaza Library. The main branch of the Brooklyn Public Library, it's situated at the north end of Prospect Park, about two and a half miles from Brooklyn Heights.

There was a large crowd on the library steps. Everyone was watching a group of amazingly talented break dancers. And standing near the front was Jeannie. We decided to creep up from behind and surprise her. When we got just a few feet from her, we began to cough loudly. Before even turning around, she managed to inform us that "It took me only forty-three minutes to walk here."

Jeannie's progress in writing the thesis was very slow. It took her six or eight months until she finally handed in the last chapter. The company was so pleased with her work that they even gave her a two-hundred-dollar performance bonus! She said it was the hardest job she had ever had.

Harry and I took her out to dinner to celebrate. Then we went to Capulets on Montague, the semi-hip neighborhood bar, where we continued our celebration.

"So, Jeannie Kaplan, MA, what will you do for an encore?"

"Howie, you're not going to believe this!"

"I think we're ready to believe anything," said Harry.

"OK, but this will test your faith."

"I'll drink to that," I declared.

"We all raised our glasses."

"To faith!" we shouted. In fact, for Harry and for me, it would be a leap too far.

95

"Are you guys ready?" We nodded.

"I got a call today from some guy with a thick Indian accent. At first I thought it was my friend Chuck, who does great accents. But this guy was really from India."

"Oh no! Don't tell me he wanted you to write another Master's thesis?"

"Close, Howie, but no cigar."

We sat there, waiting for her to tell us. But it became clear that she wanted us to guess. Harry and I locked eyes, and we both shrugged.

"Come on, you're both smart guys. Figure it out!"

We sat there trying to do just that. Then Harry began to smile. We looked at him expectantly.

"Don't tell me!"

Jeannie started laughing. Soon she was pounding the bar with her fists.

Then Harry went on. "That poor Indian guy. He was looking for someone to write his doctoral dissertation!"

"Bingo!" shouted Jeannie.

"How fucking sad," I observed.

"Sad? It's pathetic!" said Harry.

"So what did you say to the poor guy?"

"Well, Harry, I didn't know what to say. So finally I asked him how much the job paid."

"What?" we both screamed.

"Look, I felt terrible for the guy. I was just trying to be polite. I wanted to let him down easy. You know, show him that I took him seriously."

"Just out of curiosity, how much *would* they have paid you?" I asked.

"Ten dollars a page."

Harry and I busted out laughing. Ten dollars a page to write a doctoral dissertation. Un-fucking-believable!

But she was no longer smiling. Then, with a shrug, she said, "I simply couldn't *afford* to turn down such a great rate of pay."

Harry and I were suddenly stone sober. We tried talking her out of it, but she was bound and determined to take on what would clearly be a fool's errand. Besides being highly unethical, it would be virtually impossible to do. No department with a doctoral program would accept such a dissertation. As grad school dropouts ourselves, Harry and I could bear witness to just how high the bar was set. And then there was the high likelihood of getting caught.

Finally, she had heard quite enough. Without a word, she stood up and left the bar.

For weeks Harry and I checked with each other, but neither of us had heard from her. We stopped seeing her around the neighborhood, and she no longer came to the library. Finally, I tried calling her, but her phone had been disconnected. There was no way to reach her.

About a year later, a team of investigative reporters from *The New York Times* uncovered a cheating scandal involving hundreds of colleges and universities. The largest offender was a term paper mill, Academic Research Associates, which hired people to write term papers, college application essays, and even graduate theses. The story made the front page of *The Times*. And there was Jeannie's photo. She was actually smiling.

It turned out that the dissertation she had researched and written had been accepted by the sociology department of an Ivy League University. But the student who had "written" it was utterly incapable of defending his own dissertation. In fact, he could not answer even one question.

It was quickly discovered that Jeannie was the *real* author. This posed a terrible dilemma for the university. A department had accepted a dissertation that was not written by one of its doctoral candidates. This student had not written his Master's thesis or any of his term papers. The university's administrators clearly needed to resolve this dilemma as quickly as possible. So they wisely asked the Sociology Department to come up with a solution.

Within hours, the department announced that its members were so impressed with Jeannie's scholarly work that *she* would be offered a full scholarship. Since the dissertation she had researched and written had already been accepted, and she had accumulated such an impressive array of undergraduate courses, she would need just a few more courses to earn her Ph.D.

Getting Even

Are you old enough to remember when there was just one phone company? AT&T, also somewhat affectionately called "Ma Bell," controlled all long distance and local phone calls. Ma Bell charged a lot for long distance calls, but phone service was quite reliable. And while there were rumors that the company was anti-Semitic, that was just how things were in those days. Most large corporations hired few, if any Jews.

One June morning two students from Lafayette High School took the subway to downtown Brooklyn, where they had interviews scheduled with the phone company. They hoped to get summer jobs as switchboard operators.

Camille Tiberio and Barbara Goldstein had been buddies since elementary school, so it would be great if they both got hired. They were there all day, taking a written exam, a physical, and having individual interviews.

At 4 p.m., all ten of the girls who had gone through this process were sent to a small room where they would be told if they had summer jobs. A woman they had never seen before walked into the room. Consulting her clipboard, she read off the list of girls who were hired. Nine names were called.

Barbara approached the woman. "Excuse me, m'am, but I didn't hear my name called."

"What's your name?"

"Barbara Goldstein."

"Sorry, it's not on my list."

"Can you at least tell me why I wasn't hired?" asked Barbara.

"Sure. It says right here that you failed the physical."

"My God! What's wrong with me! Please tell me!"

"Look, honey, I ain't no doctor. It just says here you didn't pass the urine test."

Camille overheard this exchange. "Hey everybody! Listen up!" She had everyone's attention.

"I'm Camille, and this is Barbara. All of you are witnesses, OK?"

They all nodded.

101

"Young lady, I don't know what you're trying to do, but it's not going to work. And if you don't button your lip immediately, you're not going to be hired either."

"Well actually, you might be right if you don't hire me. You see, when we were given those bottles to pee into? Well, I couldn't pee. So Barbara poured some of her pee into my bottle."

All the girls were laughing. It wasn't hard to figure out what had happened.

"OK, Miss whatever-your-name-is: here's what you're going to do. You are going to put Barbara's name on the list. Or, if you prefer, take mine off. I'll leave that up to you. But just remember, we've got eight witnesses."

"I can't do that! I don't make the hiring decisions."

"No?" said Camille. "Then who does? Let's go to see that person right now. And that, lady, that's *your* decision."

"All right already! I can get into a lot of trouble for doing this."

"Yeah lady, but you can get into a whole lot more if you don't," said Camille.

Barbara and Camille worked for the phone company that summer, and the next one as well. When they started Brooklyn College in the fall, they laughed when they were told they needed to take a physical. "Camille, do you want me to help you study for the urine test?"

When they graduated, they both became teachers. For Camille, this would be for just a year or two. She had just gotten married, and once she started having kids, she'd let Anthony do all the breadwinning.

Barbara also had dreams. A math major as an undergraduate, she decided to go for her MA. Numbers were her thing, and even though there were very few women in her classes, she felt perfectly at home. When she got her MA, she would quit her junior high school position as soon as she could find a job teaching math at the college level.

Luck was with her; she got the first job she applied for at a college she had never heard of. In fact, almost no one had heard of the American Institute of International Studies. It had opened just a year before and its classes were held in what had once been a clothing factory near the old Brooklyn Navy Yard.

When Barbara walked into her first class, she thought she was at a session of the United Nations General Assembly. About 90 percent of the students were foreigners, many of whom spoke almost no English. Still, somehow they could work out the problems she assigned. After all, wasn't mathematics a universal language?

She was not much older than her students, but their backgrounds and hers were amazingly different. She grew up in Bensonhurst, a Brooklyn working class neighborhood that was predominately Italian, but with a large Jewish minority. In fact, the great Sandy Koufax had lived just a block away. But long before she and Camille entered Lafayette, the Dodgers had deserted Brooklyn, and he had retired from baseball.

Her students came from many different countries in Africa, Asia, South America, and a few were from Europe. In most cases, their parents made great sacrifices to send them to this great American college. Evidently they were quite impressed with the name of the school.

Most of the faculty members seemed nice enough, but she soon learned that many of them did not even have BAs, let alone graduate degrees. The administrators all seemed to be friends of the president. His father, who had made his fortune in the ladies garment industry, put up the money to start the college. The building, which he still owned, had previously housed one of his "sweat shops." Still, she *was* teaching in a college.

One day, a friend told Barbara that he had a stolen telephone credit card number. He asked her if she wanted it. "Sure. I hate the phone company."

"Why do you hate it? Because they charge so much for long distance calls?"

"Actually I have a couple of other reasons. First, I used to work for them. They treated us like shit. And the men, most of them just high school graduates—if *that* much—got paid about twice what the women made."

"So why else do you hate them?"

"Because they're fuckin' anti-Semites!"

"Barbara, I think I detect a hole in your logic."

"You mean, if they're anti-Semitic, how come they hired *me?*"

"Well yeah."

Barbara told him what had happened when she and Camille applied for summer jobs, how they took the infamous urine test, and how they both ended up working for the phone company.

"Hey, Barbara, I was aware that they can test your urine for diabetes and for kidney stones. But I never suspected that they could test it for Jewishness."

"Very funny! So while I was working there, of the hundreds of people I met, I don't remember one person who was Jewish. Oh, wait a second! There was another girl—Sheila Morse."

"That doesn't sound Jewish."

"It was changed from Moscowitz."

"She told you that?"

"Yeah, in the strictest of confidence. So now I have to kill you."

"Well before you do, Barbara, let me give you that stolen credit card number."

"Fine. And could you tell me how it works?"

"OK, I'll write down the number for you."

"516 741 9528 127K. Wow, that's long! Thirteen numbers and a letter!"

"Barbara, do you recognize the first three digits?"

"Sure, 516 is the area code for Long Island."

"The next seven digits are a phone number."

"Right! And the last three digits, 127?"

"That's the phone company's internal credit card code for the 516 area code. In other words, if the credit card number begins with 516, it has to end with 127."

"Doesn't this credit card number belong to someone?"

"Yeah, Barbara, it's actually a real person's number."

"Won't they be billed for all those calls?"

"Of course. But when they tell the phone company what happened, they won't be charged."

"Then won't the phone company go after the people making the phony credit card calls?"

"Yes, they will. So you'll need to take a couple of very simple precautions. First, use only payphones. If you use your home phone, the phone company will immediately track you down. And warn the people you call about what you're doing, so they don't give your name to anyone from the phone company."

"That's easy. How do I make the calls? And go slowly; I want to write this down."

"You put a dime in the phone. You'll get a dial tone. Dial '0', and then the area code and number you're trying to reach. When the operator comes on, tell her that you're making a credit card call. She'll say, 'Credit card number?' And you'll say, 'My number is 516 741 9528 127K.'"

"That's *it*?"

"That's it! She'll check to make sure it's a valid number, and then your call goes through. And you'll even get your dime back."

"That's fantastic! How many people did you give this number to?"

"Just a select few."

"How long is it good for?"

"Till end of the year."

"How can I thank you?"

"Do you want me to spell it out for you?"

"What, and ruin such a beautiful friendship?"

Getting that credit card number opened up all kinds of possibilities. Sure, she could make hundreds of calls to people she knew all over the country, and even in foreign countries. But that wasn't enough. She hated those anti-Semitic bastards. She needed to do a lot more.

A new semester was starting. Barbara knew what she would do. After calling the roll of her first class, she wrote the credit card number on the board. None of the students seemed to recognize what it was. Barbara just looked out at the class. Let me start by asking you a couple of questions. First, does anyone here work for the phone company?"

"Do you mean in *this* country?" asked a young man with a thick African accent. "Everyone giggled."

"Yes."

No hands were raised.

"Now for my second question: Did any of your professors ever tell you that you would learn so much from him that his class will pay for itself?"

Many of them smiled and nodded. "Please, everyone, copy down the number I wrote on the board." She watched as everyone copied it.

"Using that number, each of you will pay for this course in less than one day!"

Now everyone was smiling.

"I'm going to tell you how it's done. You need to write down all the steps."

Barbara never saw a class take such meticulous notes. Then she told them that they could call all over the world with that number. Just remember to use a pay phone, and to tell the people you call not to give your name to anyone from the phone company. In our next class, if you'd like to, you can tell us where you called.

Barbara repeated this performance in each of her other classes. When she left for the day, she was so ecstatic, she couldn't wait to tell Camille. They laughed and laughed as Barbara told her friend how she had gotten the number, how she had made all those free calls, and how she had given the number to her students.

"Barbara, I love you! So I will definitely come to visit you in jail."

Two days later, she met all her classes again. In each class, students talked about the calls they had made. Barbara kept a running tally of countries that had been called. As it approached 60, one student, who apparently was saving the best for last, now told *his* story.

"I come from a small village in India. We are all so poor that there is just one phone in the entire village. You can imagine how shocked my parents were when they were called to the phone. Neither of them had ever spoken on a phone before, nor had any of my nine younger brothers and sisters."

"So you talked to *all* of them?" asked a student.

"Why shouldn't I? Was it not a free call?"

Everyone laughed.

"How long were you on the phone?" another student asked.

"Five hours!"

"Did anyone make a longer call?" asked Barbara.

Apparently, no one had.

"Ashook! I think you hold the record!"

"Then my mother began to grow alarmed. 'This call must be costing you so much money! We must hang up the phone immediately.' No, mother, there is no rush."

Then my mother said, 'Then please explain something. If you can afford to call us from America and to talk to us for five hours, then your father and I are puzzled. Why are *we* sending *you* money?'"

Barbara estimated that her students were costing the phone company hundreds of thousands of dollars a month. Was that enough? For the phone company, it was not even pocket change. And she realized that in another few days, the credit card number would no longer be good. She needed to figure out another number that could be used for the next year. She would have to work fast.

The first thing she needed to figure out was how the operator determined if a credit card number was valid. In stores where Barbara paid by credit card, they kept a couple of books at the cash register—one for MasterCard and one for Visa. Each book had tens of thousands of stolen credit card numbers. The clerk checked your credit card number against these numbers—a process which took about a minute.

107

But when Barbara dictated the telephone credit card number to the operator, it took her just a few seconds to determine whether or not the card was valid. How did she *do* it?

It took Barbara some time, and then—*eureka!* I've got it! The operator was using a gyp sheet. If it took her only five seconds to determine whether the credit card number was valid, she could not possibly be going through a book of stolen credit card numbers.

Barbara figured that the letter must be the key, and probably just one of the thirteen numbers. OK, she thought, let's test the letter first. So she went to a phone booth. By now she had memorized the credit card number: 516 741 9528 127K. She gave the same 13 numbers to the operator, but she changed the letter to S. Five seconds later the operator said, "I'm sorry. That is an invalid credit card number."

Barbara apologized and hung up. So the letter *was* a key variable. She needed another variable to go with it. Obviously that would have to be one of the thirteen numbers. But which one? How could she figure this out?

Barbara decided to use the old trial-and-error method. She went to another phone booth and dialed a long distance number. When the operator came on, she gave the 13-digit credit card number followed by K, but she changed the first digit and kept the next 12 digits. It took the operator just a few seconds to let the call go through.

Now she made another call. She changed the second digit and the call went through. When she got to the sixth digit, which was 1, she changed it to 2. The operator then said, "That is an invalid credit card number." Bingo!

She knew now that the sixth digit was another key variable. So she went back to the original credit card number, changed each of the other twelve digits—leaving just keeping the 1 as the sixth digit—and tried to make a credit card call. The call went through.

So the sixth digit was what the operator was checking. She must have a piece of paper in front of her with the numbers from 0 to 9, and next to each of those numbers, a letter. All she was checking was the sixth digit of the credit card number to make sure the letter matched what she had on her gyp sheet. So if the sixth digit was a 1, then the letter had to be K.

So far, so good. Barbara was now sure that this year's system was based on the sixth digit and a corresponding letter. What about *next* year's credit card number? Since a credit card number is essentially someone's phone number, it would remain the same from one year to the next. Only the letter at the end of the credit card number would change. And maybe the digit chosen to be matched with that letter.

Barbara now had all the information she needed to figure out a valid credit card number when the new year began. She was pretty sure that the schmucks at the phone company would keep the same system, but probably change the digit and the letter that corresponded with it. Maybe if those anti-Semites hired a few smart Jews, they could come up with a more fool-proof system.

On January 1ˢᵗ she went to a phone booth and started making calls. Again, it would be all trial and error. She started with the same thirteen numbers that were on the stolen credit card number. And she tacked on the letter A. "I'm sorry. That's an invalid credit card number." Then she tried the letter B with the next call. And then C.

What do *you* think would be the maximum number of calls she needed to make?

You guessed it! 26 calls. And then she would be set for the entire year.

She was curious about which digit the phone company was using this year, so after just a few calls, she found that it was the fourth digit. Once you knew how the system worked, it was a piece of cake to figure out another valid number. Or another ten thousand.

So now she decided to *really* get back at those anti-Semites. She was friendly with some members of the Jewish Defense League, and it didn't take much persuading on her part to get them to give the number out to all *their* friends and families. Reach out and touch somebody? They'd reach out all right!

Barbara and her friends in the Jewish Defense League would marvel that there were two million Jews in New York, and yet if all the Jewish employees of the phone company could all meet in one room, they would not even make a minyan (a prayer group of at least ten Jewish men). Why not? Perhaps because so few Jews could pass the urine test.

Several months later Barbara spent a Sunday afternoon with Camille, her husband, Anthony, and their baby girl, Marie. They had a present for her—a book of quotations. All were attributed to President John Kennedy. Pointing at one of them, Camille told Barbara, "This quote could be your get-out-of-jail-free card. When they try to lock you up, just tell them that you were following the advice of our late president."

The quotation read, "Don't get mad. Get even."

Damaged Goods

1

Rather late one weekday evening, I saw a very attractive woman struggling to pull a huge suitcase up the subway station stairs.

"May I help you?"

She gave me the onceover, and after concluding that I did not appear to be an axe murderer, she thanked me. Ten minutes later, we were standing in front of her building. I was about to ask her for her number when she handed me her card. She was an assistant buyer for a major department store.

"You must be very important."

She laughed. "Yeah, right! If you'd like—if you can spare the time—I could tell you all about my... quote unquote... wonderful job."

"You really hate your work!"

"That would be the understatement of the year!"

"I'll tell you what. How about dinner at *Fifth and Fifth* this weekend?"

"Well, if you don't mind dining with a very tired, boring person, how about nine o'clock on Saturday night?"

"Sounds like a plan."

2

Fifth and Fifth obviously took its name from its location on Fifth Ave. at the corner of Fifth Street, in what had long been the slummy part of Park Slope, now one of Brooklyn's most desirable and expensive neighborhoods. I waited for Zoey in front of the restaurant, and she was fashionably late.

When she finally arrived and began to apologize, I waved her off.

"Zoey, trust me, you are well worth the wait!"

"That's very nice of you to say, but after the day I just had, I'm not sure I'll be very good company."

"I would rather be with you on one of your *bad* days than with most of my friends on their *good* days."

"You may want to re-evaluate after tonight."

"What happened?"

"We had our quarterly assistant buyers' day sale. The store advertises about how this is a great opportunity for its assistant buyers to show off their talents. We get to pick out the items that go on sale, and then we're on our feet for ten hours getting pinched in the ass, propositioned, and even worse things that I can't even *talk* about. And worst of all, since we get fixed salaries, we don't even get paid for the day!"

"Well, why don't we go inside and sit down? Your feet must be killing you."

"Yeah, but the rest of my body feels even worse."

"You know, I *do* give decent massages."

She smiled. "Well, maybe later. Right now, I'm starving."

3

We began seeing each other most weekends and occasionally during the week as well. Zoey worked in a five-story building across the street from the store. I waited for her in the lobby.

I noticed the guard checking the shopping bags, pocketbooks, packages, and carrying cases of the people leaving the building. That seemed kind of weird, because virtually everyone coming out of the building was an employee of the store across the street. So, the guard must have been assuming that they pilfered stuff from inside the store perhaps at lunchtime, and then brought it into this building—didn't make much sense.

Maybe the third or fourth time I was waiting for Zoey, I causally asked the guard why he was searching employees as they left the building.

"Well, some of them steal stuff from the store during their lunch hour, and then bring it back in here when they come back from lunch."

"That's pretty dumb! Especially since they must *know* that you're going to check them when they leave."

"Listen buddy, we have some pretty dumb employees!"

Just then, Zoey came out of the elevator. "Hey Jimmy, yuh gonna do another strip search?"

"Nah, you're clean! Have a nice evening."

4

We walked a few blocks to a restaurant she liked. "Do you bring *all* your beaus here?"

"Only the ones who make me split the check."

"Hey, I'm old enough to remember when we had to pay full freight."

"Yes, Steve, even I remember those good old days."

"Hard to believe!"

"Why just the other day a kindly young man asked if I'd like him to help me cross the street."

"Sounds like a pick-up line."

"You want to hear a *real* pickup line?" She paused. "Can I help you with that suitcase?'"

We both burst out laughing. Then I leaned across the table and kissed her.

The kiss seemed to last and last. Finally, both of us sensed a growing silence, and then we noticed the waitress standing near us, a big smile on her face.

Then she asked, "Where do you guys think you *are*? In *Paris*?"

"You mean, we're not?" I asked in faux disbelief.

"Actually, "added Zoey, "we really *did* come here to eat."

"Well, I'm happy to tell you that you came to the right place."

"Thank you!" said Zoey, "Could we start off with a couple of glasses of white wine?"

"And what are your specials this evening?" I asked.

We quickly ordered and then Zoey said, "Steve, I want to ask you a question, but you can definitely feel free to say 'no.'"

"Yes!"

"Great! But aren't you curious what my question is?"

"Sure!"

"OK. Would you like to come to a wedding with me?"

"Does this have anything to do with a heavy suitcase?"

She gave me a strange look. "Actually, it does!"

"Well, if the outcome is the same *this* time, then I'm definitely all in."

"Great! Then sit back, young man. This is going to be a long story."

5

It took almost an hour to fill me in on all the details. I would be just a bit player in a complicated morality play. Most of the action would take place in "the store."

Zoey and virtually all of her fellow employees referred to this very large and well-known department store as "the store." The pay was lousy, nearly all of the women working there were disparaged, and management was at best "clueless."

The assistant buyers—all of whom were young women— felt especially put upon by management, since they were forced to work long hours for relatively low salaries and were periodically called upon to do rather unpleasant tasks. Assistant buyers' days were perhaps the worst of these. There was also the unpaid overtime, the strict dress code, and the blatant sexual harassment by their "superiors," who were all males.

"Let me tell you about one especially obnoxious term that is commonly used to describe the women over thirty... Are you *ready* for this, Steve?"

I nodded.

"They call us 'career girls.'"

"Lovely."

"But that's not all, folks! Almost everybody working there is treated badly, one way or another."

"Jimmy had mentioned that there was a big problem with employee pilferage."

"Jimmy doesn't even know the *half* of it."

"Since I love listening to you, you can tell me the other half."

"Well, you are about to become indirectly involved in this. But, on the bright side, I think a good lawyer would be able to get you off without you having to do any prison time."

"With that guarantee, it appears to be a win-win situation. I'll get to play a small role in advancing the cause of social justice and get a free lunch as well."

"Actually, it's going to be a free dinner, and you will also get a free suit that will be yours to keep."

I tried to figure out where this was going. But just then, the waitress arrived with our food. We decided to table this discussion for later.

6

It was nearly midnight when we left the restaurant and headed toward my apartment. I had begun to wonder if Zoey had been a little reluctant to talk about the goings-on at work where she might be overheard. I could certainly understand how working at that place could make you a little paranoid.

As we walked up Fifth Street toward the park, Zoey squeezed my hand, which usually meant she was about to say something that required my full attention.

"Let me start at the beginning. Stores like ours receive huge shipments of men's, women's, and children's clothing. Before they are put on the floor for sale, each item is checked for any defects. Many have moth holes, quite a few are torn or stained, and occasionally, some even smell bad.

So, the manufacturer issues a credit on the defective garments. Now what do you think 'the store' *does* with this damaged clothing?"

"Sends it back to the manufacturer?"

"Good guess, Steve."

"But not good enough."

"That's right! Why bother going through expense and trouble of shipping back these damaged goods to the manufacturer? It's much easier for both parties if we just toss them."

"That makes sense!"

"Of course! But 'the store' then gives the clothing to charity and takes a tax write-off."

"So 'the store' gets a credit from the manufacturer *and* a tax write-off from the IRS. In effect then, the more damaged goods, the more profitable it is for the store!"

"Now I get it! You're going to treat me like a charity case and provide me with a damaged suit to wear to the wedding."

She squeezed my hand again.

"The suit won't actually be damaged—and it will be yours to keep."

"I actually *do* own a couple of suits, so if you're worried about my attire..."

"Oh, I forgot to ask you: Would you be willing to be in the wedding party?"

I had to think about this. Zoey waited patiently.

"Will you be in the wedding party?"

"Of course!" she answered. "You'll be an usher and I'll be a bridesmaid."

"No more questions, your honor."

Zoey smiled. "OK, here's the deal: About half the wedding party will be store employees. And 'the store' has recently been providing the wedding parties of employees with suits and dresses."

I just stared at her, my mouth wide open.

"Careful, Steve. If you keep your mouth open like that much longer, you may begin to attract flies."

"OK, I'm going to make a great intellectual leap here. Something tells me that the provision of these suits and dresses by the store is not voluntary—or even intentional."

"Why don't you come right out and *say* it, Steve? We are stealing this clothing from the store."

"Yeah! But how do you do it?"

"Well, we make it look as though we're giving them to charity. There's a big dumpster in the corner of the loading area behind the store. All the damaged clothing is brought down a freight elevator and thrown into the dumpster.

Then, in the late afternoon, one or two small trucks from the Salvation Army or another charity picks up the garbage bags of clothing, and hands the guard a receipt."

"Zoey, I can follow this so far. So, I'm guessing that you guys have arranged for your own truck to pick up your suits and dresses."

"Exactly. We even give the guard a receipt from a real charity."

"Ingenious!"

"But wait! There's more!"

"Let me guess! How will your guys know which bags to pull out of the dumpster?"

She waited to see if I could guess the answer to my *own* question. It took me several seconds, and then I smiled.

"The bags must be somewhat different from the regular garbage bags, so your guys will know which ones to fish out of the dumpster."

But then I was stuck. They couldn't put signs on the bags, "Not for charity."

Zoey waited. Finally, she decided to put me out of my misery.

"We paste big yellow stickers all over the bags. And on each sticker, in big black letters, it says, 'CAUTION! HAZARDOUS WASTE STORAGE.' And just in case anyone can't read, there's also a skull and cross-bones."

"Perfect!"

"The bags are carried down to the dumpster by two or three maintenance guys, accompanied by one of our own people who makes sure they wear gloves and hold the bags away from their bodies. Anyone who gets on the freight elevator gives them a wide berth.

The hazardous waste bags are placed in a corner of the dumpster as far as possible from the other bags. When our guys arrive, they hand a receipt to the guard, pack up their truck, and the next time those suits and dresses are seen will be at the wedding."

"I am honored to play a minor role in this grand plan. Oh! Just one more question. How will you know what size jacket and pants I wear?"

"If you're not too shy, I can take your measurements when we get to your apartment. I brought along a tape measure in case you don't own one."

7

It was a beautiful wedding! My suit fit perfectly and Zoey actually caught the bride's bouquet. One of the highlights was the last of more than a dozen toasts—To 'the store!' Without it, this wedding may have never taken place.

Many of the guests yelled, "Hear, hear!"

As the noise died down, we overheard an older woman, who spoke impeccable Brooklynese, raise an interesting question with her neighbor.

"I thought everyone *hates* the store!"

Her neighbor replied, "Tillie, it's kind of a love-hate relationship, if yuh catch my drift."

"Well anyway, it's nice they gave my Rosalind a lovely dress to wear to the wedding."

"Yeah, and my Barry, they gave him a beautiful suit!"

"So, Milly, lemma ask yuh: "What's *not* to like?"

"Well, maybe the next time that one their workers gets married, the store could spring for a better caterer."

"You're telling *me!* The food tastes like *poison!* And such small portions!"

Printing Money

1

Everything I know about printing, I learned in middle school. In the seventh grade, the boys were required to take a daily period of printing, where we learned to set individual leaden letters of type on a composing stick, and then print what we had composed. It started innocently enough with aphorisms such as "Knowledge is power," and "The worst wheel of the cart makes the most noise."

By the time my friends and I were in high school, we used our skills to print up fake elevator passes and announcements of class cancelations on days when certain exams were scheduled. To this day, I wonder how any of us ever managed to graduate.

Even after I became an economics professor, I never lost my fascination with printing. One evening, I met my nephew for dinner in a restaurant in lower Manhattan. He had recently graduated from law school and was now a lowly associate with a major Wall Street law firm.

Always in a hurry, he announced that he had to return to work in just an hour. I wondered if he was really being paid so much money, why his firm could not bear to be without him for more than an hour or two at a time.

But he surprised me by confiding that he wasn't going back to his law firm. He had pulled an all-nighter with a printer who was making multiple copies of the legal papers for a corporate acquisition that would be announced the next day. His job was to ensure that no stray copies fell into the wrong hands.

I understood immediately that anyone getting wind of this deal could make a lot of money buying shares of the stock of the company being purchased. That would constitute insider trading, which could earn either millions of dollars, or else a long prison term.

"So, you're saying that a hot stock tip is entirely out of the question?"

My nephew didn't even crack a smile. Then he shook his head, saying, "I knew I *never* should have told you!"

"Well, thank you for not killing me!"

2

A few years later, I managed to snag a contract to write a textbook, which I had great hopes of making me rich. When my book was ready to go to press, I was surprised to learn that a representative of my publisher would spend the next week at the printer's. Surely, the first edition of an introductory economics text could not possibly require a week to be printed.

My editor explained to me that that was the standard practice when major texts were being printed. While I was quite flattered that my book was already considered "major," it was puzzling why keeping the printer under twenty-four-hour surveillance was necessary. Surely, if advance word leaked out about *any* economics book, no one would ever notice, let alone profit.

Boy was I wrong! A few years before, our company published the first edition of an introductory accounting text. No one from our company was there keeping a wary eye on the printer. The initial print run was for 20,000 copies.

There had been scores of orders for the book from college bookstores across the country. But while the books were still being shipped to our warehouse, our company began receiving dozens of order cancelations.

Order cancelations were not very common, but when they *did* occur, it was because the bookstores had bought up many copies of the text from students using it the previous term. And even then, reductions in the size orders were much more common than cancelations of entire orders.

But in the case of this textbook, there were no used copies, since this was the initial printing of the first edition. So, our sales reps, who stood to lose their commissions, called the managers of every college bookstore that had cancelled its order, and a few reps even drove to the bookstores to see these books firsthand.

What do *you* think had happened? Stories like these always need a villain. So who dun it?

Well, it didn't take a Sherlock Holmes to identify the culprit. Our printer had printed thousands of extra books and sold them directly to the college bookstores.

You would have thought that some of the bookstore managers might have caught on and alerted my publisher. Of course, they had no incentive to do so. The printer had evidently charged them considerably less than my publisher did.

So, what have we learned from this sordid tale? Clearly, that printers are no more honest than other people—even lawyers and college professors.

There are two large posters displayed in the reception room of the headquarters of my publisher:

In God we trust.
All others pay cash.

If you can't trust your printer,
then whom *can* you trust?

3

Why have I told you these two seemingly unrelated stories? Well, I know that many of my students *do* refer to me as "the absent-minded professor," so clearly, I have a reputation to uphold.

As luck would have it, my involvement with printing malfeasance was not yet over. Only *this* time, it would be much more serious: It actually involved the printing of money. In fact, this was such a major economic event, that I devoted an entire page to it in my economics textbook.

I'll bet you can't guess which nation had the world's worst bout of inflation. Go ahead and make a guess. Did you guess Germany, during the 1920s?

Close, but no cigar! OK, I'll put you out of your misery. It was Zimbabwe, a very poor nation in Southern Africa. Instead of financing its government spending with tax receipts and borrowing money, the government just printed it. This set off a rapidly growing inflation.

Prices eventually were doubling every day, and the government kept printing currency with increasingly large denominations. Eventually, they printed 100,000,000,000,000-dollar bills. That is, one-hundred-trillion-dollars!

How much could even *these* bills buy? You could have gotten a pretty good idea by reading the sign posted in public outhouses throughout the Zimbabwe:

TOILET PAPER ONLY MAY
BE USED IN THIS TOILET

NO NEWSPAPER

NO CLOTH

NO CARDBOARD

NO ZIM DOLLARS

This inflation took place during the first decade of the new millennium. Finally, the government agreed to stop printing money and to no longer recognize it as legal currency. To this day, the official currency of Zimbabwe is the U.S. dollar.

So, what happened to all that Zimbabwe currency? Some was turned in to the government and destroyed. Much of it was sold abroad to foreign currency collectors. Because I had featured the Zimbabwe inflation in my textbook, I bought up about 8,000 Zimbabwe ten-trillion-dollar bills on eBay.

I paid about 50 cents for each of these bills and sent a few to each of my publisher's sales reps to offer to professors who were using my book. And better yet, I offered to supply them with enough bills for each of their students.

Amazingly, no one took me up on this very generous offer. So now I was stuck with nearly 8,000 Zimbabwe ten-trillion-dollar bills. *That* should have been the end of my story.

But then, very gradually something amazing began to happen. If you look on eBay, you'll see that these bills are selling for five or ten U.S. dollars. And I'm still holding almost 8,000 of them.

But as profitable as my investment has been, I could have done much better had I bought up the Zimbabwe hundred-trillion-dollar bills, which are now fetching between forty and one hundred U.S. dollars.

As things turned out, I was evidently not the only person who had that regret. But someone else came up with an even better idea! I don't know this person's name, but I do know that she or he must be a printer.

That's right! This printer has been turning out virtually perfect copies of the Zimbabwe $100,000,000,000,000 bills and selling them on eBay and Amazon.

Is that legal? Good question! It's certainly illegal to print your own counterfeit U.S. currency in the United States. And it may well be illegal to print the currencies of other nations such as British pounds or Euros.

But Zimbabwe currency? Because that's no longer legal currency, you're not breaking any laws by printing even one-trillion-dollar bills. It's like printing Monopoly money.

At least that's what *I* think. But I really want to be sure it's legal. So, if he's still talking to me, I'll have to ask my nephew, the lawyer.

A Case of Stolen Identity

Under the spreading chestnut tree,
I sold you and you sold me.
—from George Orwell's novel, *1984*

Chapter 1

I'm a lawyer, OK? I don't call myself an attorney because that would be much too snobby. I didn't go to one of those fancy top ten law schools. In fact, I barely got through Brooklyn Law School at night.

I'm what you call a "Court Street lawyer." I even have an office on Court Street in Downtown Brooklyn right near the courts. But calling someone a Court Street lawyer can be considered an insult. Just like calling someone a Wall Street lawyer is a compliment.

The biggest difference between these two sets of lawyers is that they get to deal with two different clienteles. The Wall Street lawyers work with corporate America and rich individuals—the big shots that run the country. We get the other ninety-nine percent. Or to be completely truthful, mostly the lower one or two percent.

There are two basic differences between their practices and ours. They get to deal with a much better class of people—and they bill three or four times as much per hour.

But us guys on Court Street? We help the *real* America—the average Joes, and sometimes the down-and-outs, too.

So one day I'm sitting in my office waiting for the phone to ring and my receptionist buzzes me.

I wait ten seconds, pretending I'm in the middle of something, and then I say, "Yeah?"

"A lady's here to see you."

"Does she have an appointment?"

"No, but she says it's urgent."

"OK, send her in."

The door opens and in walks the best-looking chick I've ever seen. And let me tell you—I've seen some real lookers.

I stood up behind my desk when she walked in. She was almost as tall as me, and I'm just a shade over six feet. OK, I'm actually five-eleven, but who's measuring?

She was wearing a beautifully tailored navy-blue pants suit that must have set her back *mucho dineros* (that's Spanish for a whole lot of money). Everything about her shouted out wealth, breeding, beauty, and maybe even a bit of street smarts. She had to know the effect she had on men, and yet, there was also a sweet innocence about her.

Her entrance reminded me of the first few lines for that classic song, "Girl from Ipanema."

Tall and tanned and young and lovely,

The girl from Ipanema goes walking,

And when she passes, each one she passes goes, Aaaah…

If she had announced that the angels had sent her to be my wife I would have gone down on one knee and proposed to her then and there.

She smiled and reached out to shake hands. Her grip was firm, and maybe it was just my imagination, but she seemed to hold my hand just a couple of seconds longer than I expected.

Our eyes locked. I knew I'd blink first. But just as I was about to, she lets go of my hand.

As anyone will tell you, doctors should never get romantically involved with their patients. And it's probably not a great idea for lawyers either. But let me be honest with you. I would have done whatever she asked me to do. And *then* some.

When she looked into my eyes, another song started playing in my head. It was kind of an old song—maybe from the eighties—and all I can remember were these two lines:

"Baby blue, were the color of her eyes.

Baby blue, like the Colorado sky."

Now I also happen to have blue eyes, but they're a couple of shades darker than hers. I couldn't help wondering what she would say if I asked her if she thought our children would inherit our blue eyes.

Now I might have a few years on her, but I work out three times a week and run in Cadman Plaza Park, which is right near the entrance to the stairs to the Brooklyn Bridge. Still, you could see at a glance that we played in very different leagues, if you catch my drift.

I mean, this babe had movie star looks, and I'm sure she'd heard that from everyone she met. Still, like that lottery ad says, "You never know."

I motioned to a chair and she sit down across from me.

I waited.

"So how can I help you, Miss…?"

"Mary Smith."

Her voice was low pitched and very sultry. In fact, if I just closed my eyes and listened, she sounded a lot like Emma Stone in *La La Land*.

"Is that your real name?"

"Why do you ask?"

"Because it sounds like a name you might make up."

"You're a very perceptive man. That's exactly why I would like to engage your services."

"What kind of case are we talking about?"

"Literary identity theft."

I felt kind of conflicted. I did not want to disappoint her, but as you might have surmised, I'm not exactly a literary lawyer. In fact, I'm more of the ambulance-chaser type. Like my fellow Court Street lawyers, I handle mostly accident, medical malpractice, divorce, and low-level criminal cases.

I figured she probably already knew that. So what did such a classy dame want with a Court Street lawyer?

I was really torn. On the one hand, I definitely did not want this woman to walk out of my life. Still, I wasn't going to lie to her.

"So how did you happen to pick me?"

"I picked you at random."

"Fair enough."

"I heard about the reputation of Court Street lawyers and I liked what I heard."

Then, almost reading my mind she added, "I hope I didn't offend you."

"No offense taken."

"Now that we have *that* out of the way, let's get down to cases," she said with a big smile.

If I wasn't already hooked, just that smile would've done the trick. I knew I would take her case no matter *what* she told me. I just hoped that she could use my services.

"By any chance, did you happen to read, *Never Again*?"

"I really don't have much time for reading. So, it's fiction?"

"Yes. In fact, it was reviewed by *The New York Times*, the *Washington Post*, and several other major newspapers."

"Holy shit! You must be famous!"

She smiled.

"No offense," I blurted out.

"None taken. But to set the record straight, I was not the author of that book. I was just curious if you had heard of it. Actually, the reason I'm here is to talk to you about another book by the same author."

"So tell me about this book. But remember, I'm no great literary expert."

"As far as I know, the author will give the final draft to his publisher within weeks."

"OK," I said. "Let me guess: You are offended by something in the book?"

"Yes, definitely!"

"And it was the part that was written about *you*."

"Bingo!"

"Now I may be going a little beyond my depth, but is what you're saying that the author lied about you and made you look bad?"

"Not at all! Not only was everything about me truthful, but he literally stole my identity to write the book."

"So it's a biography?"

"No, it's a novel. But I would agree that there are major biographical elements. After all, in order to write the book, he felt compelled to steal my life."

"OK," I said, but not really following what she was saying, or why she wanted to sue.

She noticed my confused expression and was trying not to laugh out loud.

I had no idea how I could help her, but even if I hadn't desperately needed the business. I knew that I would take her case.

"So you're not suing because he wrote bad things about you that weren't true?"

"Correct."

"Then could you please explain to me exactly why you're suing him?"

"I'll try. But you'll need to suspend your disbelief."

I was quite ready to suspend my disbelief or anything else just to keep her sitting there. So I buzzed my receptionist and told her to hold all my calls. Then I paused a few seconds and added, "And cancel my eleven o'clock!"

Then I sat back, smiled, and said, "I'm all ears, Ms. Smith."

"Before we begin, do you understand that what I am about to tell you must be kept strictly confidential?"

"Of course! Even Court Street lawyers are bound by that rule."

"So, you will never repeat anything that I tell you unless I give you my explicit permission? And certainly not to the police."

"Again, it would not only be unethical for me to do so, but I would likely be disbarred."

"Alright then. Let me put things *this* way: Despite appearances, I am a criminal."

"OK."

"That doesn't surprise you?"

"In this line of work, *nothing* surprises me."

"Excellent! But don't worry, I didn't kill anyone."

"Whooooh! You sure took a load off my mind!"

She smiled. "What I did do was steal."

"What did you steal?"

"Pennies."

"Why bother?"

"I stole hundreds of thousands of pennies every day."

"Fuck me!"

135

I tried to stammer out an apology, but she burst out laughing. Then she tried to explain.

"I'm sorry! It was just the apologetic expression on your face."

"Well, I'm sorry for the outburst, but you really took me by surprise."

"Would you like to hear how I managed to steal all that money?"

"I'm all ears."

For the next two hours, she told me how she did it. A lot of it involved computer programs, very complicated calculations, and some kind of statistical gibberish. In short, I couldn't follow most of what she was telling me.

Around noon I sent out for sandwiches and then went through the motions of canceling the rest of the day's appointments. Then I gave her a slight nod and sat back to listen.

Amazingly, once the math and computer crap were out of the way, she actually began to make sense. She must have finally realized that I had not been making heads or tails of what she had been saying.

"Let's begin with a basic fact: Most people don't care about pennies. When you're in the store paying for something and you're a penny short, they tell you to forget about it. If the price of something is a penny more than you thought it was, it doesn't make any difference. And there are a lot of people who, if they drop a penny in street, don't bother to pick it up."

I knew firsthand that she was right. Except that I usually *do* stoop down to pick up any pennies that I drop.

Then she handed me a card with some tiny, printed numbers and asked me to read them.

I don't happen to use reading glasses, but I know that I probably should. I held the card about two feet away and read, "Eighty-eight dollars and ninety-nine cents."

"Close, but no cigar."

"Really?"

"Look again."

I squinted.

"It *still* looks like eight-eight ninety-nine."

"Try using your cell phone."

I pulled it out and shined the light on the card.

"Eighty-eight ninety-eight?"

"Right you are!"

"How big is that font?"

"Remember the old phone books?"

"Sure."

"It's the same font as in the white pages."

"Wow!"

"So you can see how easy it is to make mistakes."

"Of course."

"Now if the mistakes were in dollars, hundreds of dollars, or certainly in *millions* of dollars, that would be a lot more likely to attract attention."

"Would you believe I once deposited a thousand dollars in my bank account and the jerks recorded it as a hundred. I found out about it pretty quickly because they sent me a notice saying that I was overdrawn.

"So I went to the bank and demanded to see the manager. I had my deposit slip with me. He corrected their mistake, but the schmuck didn't want to cancel the overdraw fee."

"I'll bet you gave him a piece of your mind."

"You'd be right."

"Moving right along," she said, "if someone here and someone there is short one penny on a transaction, almost none of them will notice. And of those who do, they probably won't care. Oh, and one more thing. Have you ever heard of a rounding error?"

"It sounds familiar, but I'm not really sure what it is."

"Well, I'll give you an easy one. Round off the number 2,351 to the nearest thousand."

I had to think about that for a few seconds. "2,000? Did I get it right?

"I got it right?"

"You sure did. The thing with rounding errors is that sometimes people round up when they should round down, or vice versa."

"Sure, I can see how easy it would be to make that mistake."

"OK, so suppose your employer rounds off your weekly pay to the nearest dollar so she doesn't have to deal with change. By mistake she might round it up when she should have rounded it down."

"Or down, when she should have rounded it up."

"Exactly."

When the sandwiches arrived, she insisted upon paying for them. She handed the guy a hundred-dollar bill and told him to keep the change.

"Boy! If I knew you were picking up the check, I would've ordered the deluxe."

"Do you mean to tell me counselor, that you would have done so even though you know that your lunch was paid for with stolen money?"

"Well, I hate to tell you, but it wouldn't have been the *first* time."

Even though she was a class chick, she certainly wasn't snooty. On the other hand, where on the social scale do you rank a person who steals?

Still, I can tell you from my professional experience that *everybody* steals—the rich, the poor—and all the people in between. Of course, very few of the big ones ever get caught.

I wondered how much she had stolen. Probably in the millions—or even more.

After a few bites, she continued her story. I guess this was going to be a business lunch, so I could bill the time.

"I worked for a very large investment bank in the financial district. I majored in computer science at Columbia and picked up a masters in statistics a couple of years later. The bank paid my tuition."

"Nice."

"Anyway, many of the guys I worked with were sexist assholes, so they didn't take me seriously."

"And you used their sexism against them."

"Exactly."

For the rest of the afternoon she explained in great detail how she was able to pull off her scheme. Her bank was a member of a huge clearinghouse that handled billions of financial transactions every business day. These included payments for everything from rent checks and income tax refunds to multibillion-dollar business deals.

Her department worked directly with the computer operations staff at the clearinghouse. Her job was to create the software they used to facilitate payments to and from her bank.

Each day as hundreds of millions of payments flowed into her bank, she was able to skim one penny from many of them.

"Why not from *all* of them?" I asked.

"A couple of reasons. First, I needed to eliminate every payment that ended with two zeroes."

"I get it! The payee would notice."

"Right you are! The second reason was that the payee might also notice if any regular monthly payments deviated by even one penny."

"And you were able to write a program that would exclude these types of payments?"

"Well, it's not quite as easy as that sounds, but essentially, yes."

"So then, after eliminating the payments that end in zero-zero and the regular monthly payments, did you skim a penny from the other ninety or ninety-five percent of the payments?"

"Not at all! I skimmed from just one percent of them."

"Why not skim from *all* of them?"

"Excellent question."

I was very pleased with myself. I guess she'd noticed because she let me enjoy the moment before she went on.

"There were two reasons why I didn't steal a penny from each of the payments. First, why be so greedy? And second, I wanted to minimize my chances of getting caught. Someone might notice a pattern if I skimmed from every payment. But it's exceedingly unlikely that anyone would notice a pattern if a penny went missing from just one of every one hundred payments."

"Interesting. Most of the criminals I've dealt with would have tried to grab every penny. And that's how they usually got caught!"

Then I asked about the other people in her department. She was the only woman and they basically left her alone to do her own thing. That was fine with her, because even if her operation were discovered, she would be the last person suspected.

"But you designed the system!"

"I did. But my boss took all the credit."

"So, was your scheme discovered?"

"I don't think so. I can't be sure. You see, I'm no longer with the bank."

We sat there in silence, while I let it all sink in. I was about to tell her my fee schedule, but she must have been a mind reader. She reached into her bag and handed me a letter sized envelope. It was pretty thick.

"I think you will find this an adequate advance payment. I'm not currently in a position to sign a contract. But here's my card so we can keep in touch."

The name on it was Mary Smith, and it had a phone number and an e-mail.

"Do you work with a private investigator?" she asked.

"Yes, of course."

"A man or a woman?"

"A man. Nearly all of them are men."

"Well, this will be for him once he's engaged." She handed over another envelope.

"So where do we go from here?" I asked.

"Well, I'd like you to sleep on it. And if you're still interested, we can talk further tomorrow."

"Sounds good to me."

After she left, I opened the first envelope. It contained a pile of hundreds. I didn't bother to count.

Chapter 2

I called her in the morning and thanked her for her generosity. She graciously accepted my thanks, and we agreed to meet again the next day at her apartment.

I was very surprised to learn that she lived in Park Slope. I mean, who-da figured her for a Brooklyn girl?

Her building was on a beautiful tree-lined block just off Seventh Avenue, the main shopping drag. It was a four story townhouse. She buzzed me in and I climbed three steep flights of stairs. There appeared to be one apartment on each floor.

She was waiting at the top of the stairs and thanked me for coming. I thought maybe she would give me the grand tour, but instead just gave me some time to look around.

Her apartment took up the fourth floor, and consisted almost entirely of open space, with a kitchen, bathroom, and bedroom at one end.

There was a dining area and workspace, but aside from a couple of white leather couches and a recliner, there was no other furniture. Of course, she had only recently moved in—and had brought virtually none of her possessions.

We sat at a table in what served as the dining area and she asked me if I'd like a cup of coffee.

"Yeah, if it's not too much trouble."

"If it were too much trouble, why would I have made the offer?"

"Nice comeback."

She brought everything in on a tray, and then we got right down to business. She had been married for seven years to a guy she had met in college.

"Columbia, right?"

"Yes. Mike was an English lit major, and an aspiring writer. We were still dating after we graduated, and he went on to get an MFA."

"That's some kind of masters?"

"Yes, a Master of Fine Arts. A lot of writers feel it's not just very helpful training, but also a good credential."

"Credential for *what?*"

"Sometimes I've wondered about that myself. Either you can write or you *can't* write."

"And Mike?"

"His writing was one of the things that made me fall in love with him."

"Did he write you love poems?"

"He did, indeed."

"So the two of you have been married for seven years?"

"Let me put it this way: We were in love *before* we got married. We were in love for the first five or six years of our marriage. And then things started to go downhill."

I realized right then that her husband must have been the reason she had hired me. Maybe she needed a good divorce lawyer. While that's not my forte, I *have* handled three or four cases.

"Did you think there was another woman?"

"Not at first. After all, I was working long hours and he was at home writing. I doubt very much that he was fooling around on the side. I can't tell you just how serious he was about his writing."

"Was he successful?"

"That depends on your definition of success."

"Well, did he sell stuff? Did he make a living?"

"At first—maybe for the first couple of years of our marriage—he had about six or eight short stories published in some fairly well-known literary magazines. He was very proud when he got his first check—for one hundred dollars."

"So these writing credits were actually more credentials? Maybe like getting a couple of different colored belts in karate."

"Yeah, I can definitely see the analogy. If you got yourself published in some of the more prestigious literary magazines, you were much more likely to get a contract from a good publishing house for your novel."

"So he was getting close."

"Well, his chances seemed to be getting better and better. And then he began writing what he called 'the Great American Novel.'"

"That was the title?"

She laughed. Maybe it *should* have been. No, in the literary world many writers aspire to write such a book—a book that all the literary critics, and a large majority of academics and serious readers would consider the greatest American novel ever written. But none of them has succeeded."

"Not even John Grisham or Tom Clancy?"

"No, not even *those* masters."

We both chuckled.

"But yesterday, you told me that Mike wrote something that might become a best seller."

"Indeed, I did."

"So maybe someday that book could at least be in the running for becoming the Great American Novel."

"Perhaps," she agreed. "But getting back to his *first* book, the more Mike wrote, the more encouraged he became."

"So did he find a publisher?"

"Not right away. But a very well-respected literary agent took him on."

"And he found a publisher who would give him a big advance?"

"Well, with fiction, publishers like to see the whole manuscript before they agree to sign a contract and provide an advance."

"Except for John Grisham and Tom Clancy."

"Exactly."

"And Mike didn't have a big name yet."

"Are you *sure* you're not a literary lawyer?"

"You can *bank* on it," I said with a smile.

"So, when Mike had most of it written, his agent shopped it around. At first there were just a few nibbles, but not one bite.

"So Mike kept writing. And then, just as he was adding the finishing touches, a major publishing house signed him."

"How much was his advance?"

"Twenty-five thousand dollars."

"Not too shabby."

"We went out to celebrate. It was right around our fifth wedding anniversary. So we had a double celebration."

"And then what happened?"

"Well, we had been putting off having a baby. But now that Mike was on his way, and I was starting to make a good salary at the bank, we decided to give it a shot."

"Say, before you tell me more, this might be a good time to take a break."

"Great idea. How about a stroll in the park? It's just a couple of blocks from here."

Prospect Park is the largest park in Brooklyn, unless you count Marine Park, most of which isn't a real park. It's more like swampland and brush. I told Mary that our high school track team used to practice in Prospect Park once a week every fall.

"The coach wanted us to get some practice running up and down hills. Maybe every other Saturday morning, we'd go to Van Cortlandt Park which is way up in the Bronx. We would run in cross country meets."

"How far did you run?"

"Two and a half miles. The coach used to tell us to let our momentum running down a hill help carry us up the next hill."

"That makes a lot of sense."

"Yes, it does."

"Do you still run?"

"Yeah, but now I run by myself in Cadman Plaza Park."

"Where is that?"

"It's just a few blocks from my office. If you were to walk north along Court Street past Montague, you'd see it on your right."

"Brooklyn is still very new to me. Before I moved here— which was just two weeks ago— I doubt if I had been to Brooklyn more than two or three times."

"So you're not from New York."

"Well, that depends upon what you mean by 'New York.'"

"The city."

"Why not the whole state?"

"You must be from upstate."

"As a matter of fact, I am."

"Where?"

"A small town outside Albany."

"I guess that could also be considered New York."

"Thanks a lot!"

"Don't mention it.

"So you got a scholarship to Columbia?"

"How did you know?"

"Simple deduction. Yesterday, you mentioned that your company paid for your graduate school. And you also said that you and Mike put off having a family until you could afford it."

"And, as you also know, counselor, I steal pennies."

"Mary, I think it would be OK for you to call me Charlie."

"So, Charlie, does *your* family still live in New York?"

"No, my parents moved to South Florida. And my brother and his family live out on the Island."

"Long Island?"

"Yeah."

"Well isn't Long Island in New York? Like Albany is?"

"Mary, you're confusing the city with the state. In the city, when we say 'New York,' we're referring to city. So if you live in one of the five boroughs, then you live in New York. If you live north of the city, you live upstate. And Long Island? That's the island."

"That makes no sense!"

"Maybe not to an apple knocker."

"A *what*?"

"An apple knocker is a person who lives upstate."

"I never heard that term before."

"Google it."

She took out her phone and typed. Then she started smiling.

"Google provides two definitions, so take your pick: The first one is 'a person who picks or sells apples.'"

"That sounds about right. What's the second definition?"

"An ignorant or unsophisticated person."

"Why don't we go with the first?"

"Thank you very much!"

"You've never heard the term before?"

"Well, what do *you* think? That we upstaters call ourselves apple knockers?"

"I guess not."

"Anyway, I left there to go to school and I never looked back. But you still have friends you grew up with?"

"Yeah, a few. But I'm still in Brooklyn. Almost everyone else either moved to the suburbs or other parts of the country."

"Where do you live?"

"I used to live in the Heights. But my landlady got an offer she couldn't refuse, so I had to move. I've been living in Carol Gardens for the last few years."

"I've heard that Carol Gardens is nice."

"It is. But it ain't the Heights—*or* the Slope, for that matter."

"I like the Slope. It's pretty quiet, and I never run into anyone I used to know."

"Does that have anything to do with your husband?"

"It has *everything* to do with him."

"OK, why don't we go back to the time when he got that nice advance and you went out to celebrate."

"Yes, I can tell you all about it at lunch. I know an excellent pizzeria. They say they have the best pizza in Brooklyn."

"Boy, do *you* have a lot to learn!"

Half an hour later, we were sitting in the backyard of the greatest pizzeria in all of Brooklyn. There were about twenty picnic tables of different sizes and even a tall oak tree providing ample shade. We had ordered a pie with pepperoni and sausage.

"So is this great pizza or what?"

"Well, before we get to that, permit me to observe that you're cutting up your slice and eating it with a knife and folk."

"Isn't that the way it's supposed to be eaten?"

"Where have you been?" I asked.

"So you mean *you're* eating it the correct way?"

"The *only* way! Look around."

She did. Then she picked up another slice, folded it half, and took a big bite.

"Charlie, I hate to tell you…"

"Yeah?"

"You're right! It actually *does* taste better this way!

"So what do you think, Charlie, isn't this great pizza?"

She looked at me expectantly.

"It's OK."

"Just OK?"

"Yeah. OK as in not bad… but nothing great."

"I see."

"Yuh need to sample the pizza all over Brooklyn, and in the city too. Alotta pizzerias claim theirs is the greatest, but they can't *all* be right."

"Exactly. Just like not every writer can write the Great American Novel," she said.

"And maybe, not even *one* writer."

"Maybe not."

She seemed to grow contemplative. I waited until she was ready to talk.

"Looking back, I would say that not long after our fifth anniversary celebration, things began to go downhill. But I barely noticed, and I doubt that Mike did either."

"Well, what might have been the first indication?"

"Probably about six months later, when Mike's book was published."

"Was it successful?"

"We thought it was—at least at first. The book was fairly widely reviewed, and most of the reviews were good."

"Did he go on an author's tour around the country?"

"The so-called author's tour is a tremendous myth, Charlie. Unless your book is published by a big house and they really get behind it. But nearly all publishers do virtually nothing to promote their books. Maybe one one-hundredth of one percent of all published novelists are sent on book tours. The rest of them are pretty much left to arrange their own publicity."

149

"So that's what happened to Mike?"

"Well, not right away. The publisher's publicist got him on a few local radio shows and a few call-in shows from out of town. The book was initially selling a few hundred copies a week—which was not nearly what we were hoping for.

"Then he started doing readings in small independent bookstores—and a couple of Barnes and Noble stores. We invited our friends, but there were very few people in the audiences. After a few months we gave up."

"Did Mike get depressed?"

"It's hard to say. He has always been very low key, but in hindsight, he may have been."

"You mentioned wanting to have a baby."

"Well, as you might have guessed, we stopped talking about that and just tried to carry on as if nothing happened. Except for one thing."

"Which was what, Mary?"

"My penny scheme."

"You put it into action?"

"Actually, I had been doing it for almost two years. I had started on just a very small scale, skimming just a few hundred dollars a day. By now my take was up to more than ten thousand."

"Did Mike know?"

"No, I didn't tell him. I was planning on surprising him, maybe when I got pregnant. I kept the money in numbered accounts I had set up overseas."

"It's hard for me to wrap my mind around your stealing all those pennies from your bank."

"Did you think that I waited until everyone was asleep each night and that I carried out large sacks of pennies?"

"So everything was done electronically?"

"Of course. That's how banks move money these days. But I actually took it a step further. Every day, after I moved the money, I deleted all the transactions."

"Is there any way they could trace what you did?"

"There's *always* a way. What I tried to do was minimize the odds of their even discovering that any money was stolen—let alone finding the culprit."

Just then the waitress came over. "Are you guys still working on that?" We looked at each other.

"No, I guess not," I said. "Could you wrap it for us?"

When we returned to her apartment, we settled into two very comfortable easy chairs and she continued her story.

"Mike had already made a start on another novel, but I think even *he* knew he'd have a lot of trouble getting a contract, let alone a decent advance."

"How did *you* feel, Mary?"

"You mean about his publishing prospects or about him?"

"Both, I suppose."

"Well, I tried to be supportive. We had both invested so many years in this quest."

"The quest to write the Great American Novel?" I asked with a grin.

"No, really just a successful writing career. Mike was certainly good, but was he good *enough*?"

"What do you think now? After all, the man has written a possible bestseller."

"Charlie, you have just uncovered the reason why I came to see you."

"I'm not sure I follow."

"I can promise you that you will very soon."

I didn't have a clue where this was going, but she certainly had aroused my curiosity. Besides, you'll never hear me complaining about hanging out with a beautiful woman who was paying me very handsomely for my time.

Chapter 3

We met again the next day. Mary asked if I had engaged a private investigator. I had indeed: Dan and I had worked together for years. He was thorough, honest, reliable, and kept his mouth shut.

Mary was delighted with my description of Dan. After she'd filled me in on the last two years of her marriage, she thought that would be a good time for Dan to join us, perhaps even the next day. But I wasn't yet sure why she would need Dan's services.

Then Mary continued her story.

"We began growing further and further apart. I had now set up several numbered bank accounts in Switzerland and the Cayman Islands."

"And Mike knew nothing."

"No, I opened a safe deposit box at another bank, and kept the key in my desk at work."

"And he never found out?"

"Actually, he *did*."

"How did he react? I mean, here you were making hundreds of thousands—

"No, millions."

"Wow, OK, millions of dollars—and he was a poor starving writer."

"Yeah, right!"

"But you *did* support him for seven years. Not many spouses would have done that."

"Oh, I don't know about that," said Mary. "Look at all the poor wives who put their husbands through medical school, and even beyond."

"Yeah, but at least there's a payoff when Mister MD starts making the big bucks."

"That's true. Still, betting on a fiction writer is much less likely to pay off."

"Right! But Mike may end up writing a bestseller," said Charlie.

"That is certainly a possibility."

"Mary, am I reading something between the lines? Something that maybe isn't quite kosher?"

"Now whatever can you mean? I'm just a naïve *shiksa* from out of town—and an apple knocker to boot."

I loved listening to her mock me. I waited for her to elaborate. There certainly *was* something there between the lines.

"Now, Charlie, we come to the dramatic twist in this sordid tale. You better buckle your seatbelt.

"As you can imagine, my skimming scheme was a fairly complex operation, something I could not manage at work."

"So you needed to work from home."

"Not entirely, but I did do the bulk of it at home."

"And Mike realized what you were doing."

"Well, he certainly did not have the computer background— let alone the mathematical background—to figure out what I was up to."

"Did he have your password?"

"I never bothered to use one. And besides, even if he snooped, he would have no idea what I was working on."

"So how did he find out?"

"Well, first, let me tell you how I found out he knew. And then we can work our way back to how *he* found out."

"Boy, you're starting to sound like John Grisham."

"Let's not get carried away."

"OK, I'm all ears."

"Around the time of our seventh anniversary—which, incidentally, we didn't bother to celebrate—Mike made me an offer I couldn't refuse. If he did not write a successful novel within the next six months, he would go out and get a real job, and we could finally start a family."

"How did you feel about this?"

"I felt that it was too late to save our marriage. I was planning on leaving him sooner than that. But, hey, why not give it a shot? He said that he had a great idea, and already had an outline and about half the book written. He was on a roll. And his mood had certainly improved."

"And this would turn out to be his alleged bestseller?"

"Correct. Well a few months went by and he was certainly firing on all cylinders. There was just one problem: He refused to tell me anything about the new book."

"Did this arouse any suspicions?"

"Maybe not immediately. But he had always asked me to read parts of his manuscripts aloud so he could hear how they sounded. I liked doing that because it made me part of his writing process."

"So now he was shutting you out. Were you OK with this new approach?"

"I guess I was. He said that he wanted to present it to me as a finished work."

"So you weren't resentful or suspicious?"

"Honestly?" She paused and thought about this for several long seconds. Then she concluded, "Whatever floats your boat."

"Sounds like you didn't give a shit."

"And you'd be correct. Mike was a damn good writer, but I was getting sick and tired of supporting him. I felt like a complete fool."

She seemed to be withdrawing, lost in her own thoughts, so I excused myself and told her I needed to check my appointments and would return as soon as I could.

A half an hour later, we were working again. I tried to sum things up.

"You were not at all suspicious about Mike's big mood swing and didn't much care. I'd like to hear how you discovered how he had stolen your identity."

"Fine. We'll cut right to the chase. You want to know how I discovered that Mike was on to my skimming operation."

"Right."

155

"One afternoon when Mike was out, I went into his office to pick up the recycling papers from his wastepaper basket. We were a very environmentally concerned couple.

"Mike kept a clear plastic bag inside the basket, so all he had to do was tie the top and it was ready for the garbage."

"That's a good idea."

"Actually, it is. Mike also liked playing garbage pail basketball."

"Me too! In fact, I'm deadly from ten feet in."

"So was Mike. There were all these balled up pages in the basket. When I pulled the plastic bag out of the basket, I noticed that he missed a shot. I picked up this balled-up piece of paper, and for some reason I smoothed it out. It was a typed page he had discarded after he had edited it by hand. This was a page from his secret novel. I decided to fish though the bag and found a few other pages."

"And you discovered that his so-called 'novel' was actually all about your penny-skimming scheme."

"Well played, Charlie."

"Lucky guess."

"Lucky guess my ass!"

I doubled over laughing. Then she was laughing too. We kept laughing and laughing, but neither of us had any idea what was so funny.

Then I had another question: "What do you think aroused Mike's suspicions that led him to go snooping on your computer?"

"Actually, I have two theories."

"Let me guess, Mary. The first theory was whether you were cheating on him."

"Which I wasn't—although I can't say I wasn't tempted."

"And the second?"

"This one is a little more complicated. You see, when Mike writes, he gets into the minds of his characters."

"OK."

"For years, he had been listening to my complaints about my job—about how I was underpaid and underappreciated. So *why* did I stay there for over seven years?"

"Yeah, but your seven years of marriage could not have always been a bed of roses, and you hadn't left *that* either. Mike may have concluded that you were a masochist."

"True, but our marriage was pretty good for most of the first five years. Still, I often wondered why I was supporting a man who probably could have gotten a decent job teaching English composition and literature to college freshmen."

"Well anyway," I said, "maybe he figured out that you could have had some reason that was keeping you at a job you didn't like. Maybe there was some incentive."

"I'm inclined to agree."

"So if that's the case," I concluded, "we don't need to know for sure what his motivation was —a suspicion that you were having an affair or that there was something fishy going on at the bank. What we *are* sure of is that he went into your computer and poked around."

"Exactly."

We decided to call it a day while we were still ahead. We needed Dan to hear the rest of the story, so I gave him a quick phone call and arranged for the three of us to gather in my office the next morning at ten a.m.

Chapter 4

When Mary first laid eyes upon Dan, I could see that she was holding herself back from bursting into laughter. In his fifties, with a florid complexion, a full head of gray hair, and twinkling blue eyes, he was the very image of a department store candidate for Santa Claus, aided by the fact that he of medium height and a good forty pounds overweight. He had an unlit cigar in his mouth and flashed a big smile.

Dan was wearing a brown suit that had long since fallen out of fashion, with the jacket unbuttoned to accommodate his ample gut. His trousers looked like they could have used a good pressing, and his shoes were scuffed. Mary told me later that he reminded her of a large unmade bed.

When she walked into the room he stood, extended a meaty paw and said, "Good tuh meet yuh! Charlie didn't tell me how beautiful you were. I hope you don't take that as sexual harassment or anything."

"Compliments like yours are always welcome. So what's with the cigar?"

"Twenty years ago the missus threatened tuh leave me if I didn't quit smokin."

"So why do you still have a cigar?"

"I dunno. Anyways, as long as I got one in my mouth, I don't need to actually smoke—if *that* makes any sense. So whadda 'bout you, Mary? Did you ever smoke?"

"No."

"Yeah, you and Charlie both. A new generation of abstainers."

Mary gave Dan a look, not sure exactly what he might be getting at—if anything.

I watched this exchange with some amusement. Then I clapped my hands and said, "Mary, Dan, let's get down to cases, as it were."

We took seats around my tiny conference table. I told Mary that Dan had been brought up to speed, so we were now ready to break new ground: "Mary, if it's OK, Dan has a few questions for you."

"Shoot!" said Mary.

"Mary, once you discovered that your husband had gotten into your computer and was writing a story based on stuff he found, what were you thinking?"

"You mean after my rage subsided?"

"Yeah."

"How the hell was he able to *do* it?"

"Did he have your password?"

"I didn't use one. As you know, there were just two places he would have looked—in my emails and my documents."

"OK."

"If he went through my emails—even if he were snooping to see if I was seeing some other guy—he wouldn't have found anything."

"Were you seeing some other guy?"

"No."

"What was in your documents?"

"Mainly stuff that he might have thought was work-related. I work in the computer operations of a large bank, mainly writing programs."

"I sure as hell wouldn't have been able to make heads or tails out of that gibberish."

"And neither could Mike. Not in a million years!"

"How do you think he found out about what you were doing?" asked Dan.

"He had to have gotten help. In fact, it could have cost him thousands—or even tens of thousands of dollars."

"Now, the guy was a writer, and you were his sole source of support?"

"That's correct. Except for a $25,000 advance he received a few years ago, he had no income whatsoever."

"OK, let's backtrack for a minute. Since Mike could not understand what you had written in these documents, he would have needed outside help—and that help would cost him a pretty penny."

"Right."

"Would he have had the person come to your apartment when you were at work? Or maybe he used a zip drive to copy your files?"

"I'd guess he used a zip drive. You see, whomever he hired would have needed to spend hundreds of hours deciphering what I had written. And he would have had to have gone through dozens of documents."

"In other words, there were no executive summaries that some knowledgeable person could have read—and then concluded, 'ah *ha!*' Now I see what she's up to!'"

"Definitely not."

"Excellent. We've pretty much established that Mike hired an expert who charged him what... tens of thousands of dollars? Mary, the last thing anyone would ever need to advise you—of all people—would be to follow the money."

We all smiled.

"You want to know if I had looked at our credit card bills and joint checking account statements for larger-than-unusual withdrawals during this period?"

"You're a regular mind reader," said Dan.

"I opened a post office box and arranged to have duplicates of the last three years of our credit card and checking account records sent there."

"Excellent. Did Mike handle the family finances?"

"He did."

"How well did he handle the money?"

"Fairly well. He always paid off our credit card balances every month, so that there were no late fees. And he kept our money at a bank that paid relatively high interest rates."

"Did you own other financial securities?"

"We had a portfolio of five blue chip stocks which we slowly added to over most of our marriage."

"Did the two of you ever sell any of these?"

"No, Mike had a theory that if you hold on to your blue chip stock long enough, you'll end up tripling or quadrupling your money."

"So you were very careful to make sure that Mike didn't know that you were studying the family finances," asked Dan.

"That's right."

"Do you still have all the records?"

Mary handed him a large envelope and gave another envelope to me.

"These contain all the bank statements, credit card, and stock records that I sent for."

"What I'd like to do, Mary, is take a close look at these before we discuss them any further."

"Of course."

I was very pleased with the way things were going and had little to add. Clearly Mary and Dan had hit it off, and I even began to wonder if there was any reason to feel a little jealous. On the other hand, maybe Mary gave me a few points for bringing Dan into the case.

Dan decided that we needed a little change of pace, so he shifted the conversation to how Mary liked living in Brooklyn compared to the city, and how it felt to be someone who had apparently disappeared off the face of the Earth.

When we were ready to break for lunch, I suggested a Syrian restaurant on Atlantic Avenue. Dan observed that I knew more about Middle Eastern food than anyone else he knew.

"You see, Mary, every so often Dan *does* get something right'" I said as we headed to Atlantic Avenue.

Chapter 5

The meal was purely social. Having eaten in all the Syrian restaurants in the area, I felt qualified to explain that locally, Syrian, Arabic, and Middle Eastern food were all one and the same.

"So why are you calling it Syrian food?" asked Mary.

"Probably because seventy or eighty years ago, when a substantial number of Arabs settled in the neighborhood, the largest group came from Syria."

"So this food we're eating is not specifically Syrian?"

"That's right, Mary. In fact, the family that owns this place is actually from Lebanon."

"Very strange!"

"Mary, you want strange? To show you what an expansive view some of these people have of their culture, let me tell you about a conversation I overhead last week.

One guy asked another guy, 'Are you an Arab?'

The other guy smiled, shook his head, and said, 'No, I am a Puerto Rican.'

And the first guy—without missing a beat—said, 'Same thing!'"

Dan started laughing, while Mary just shook her head.

When we returned to the office, I made a show of picking up a handful of messages from my receptionist, glancing at them, and then stuffing them in my pocket. Well, "nice try" I thought to myself when I caught Dan's wink at Mary and her wink back.

As soon as they were seated around the table in the conference room, Dan wanted to focus on the computer expert Mike had hired.

"Mary, would you say that what the computer expert found would be a blueprint for ripping off a bank?"

"That would depend on how good the expert was and how much time was spent going through my documents."

"So you're saying that there was no step-by-step plan laid out?"

"Not at *all!* These were notes to myself. The step-by-step plan was in my head. I had no need to write it down."

"How easily would the computer expert have been able to put all the pieces together?"

Mary needed to think about this. Dan and I waited patiently while she mulled this over.

Then she blurted out, "Simple deduction!"

"Go on," said Dan, encouragingly.

"Let me give you an analogy. Suppose you saw a sketch of a bank lobby with arrows pointing to where the guard was stationed, and where the alarm buttons and the cameras were located."

"I would guess that someone might be planning a bank robbery."

"Very good, Charlie," said Dan. Maybe you should be doing *my* job."

"Moving right along," said Mary, "what any computer expert worth her or his salt would quickly conclude was that someone was fixing to rob a bank—but without using a gun.
That's why I could not have worked out my plan at the bank. If they *did* discover that they had been robbed, the first place they'd have looked would have been their employees' computers."

Dan and I looked at each other. We were both getting the picture. It was becoming very clear that Mike must have gotten a lot of help from someone who knew a thing or two about computers.

Dan then asked Mary, "So do you think that any person who was knowledgeable about computers would be able to figure out your scheme?"

"No, certainly not just *any* person. But I would say almost any computer expert with a decent imagination. Someone who could connect the dots. There certainly wasn't a step-by-step plan."

"OK, then let's shift gears. Your husband learned what your plan was. And he was able to write about it in layman's terms for the average reader."

"Yes, I must say that I was rather impressed."

"He must have been on to you for some time while the two of you were still together, right?"

"Yes, he was."

"And he never let on?"

"No."

"Do you think he knew that you had actually carried out your plan and were skimming money from the bank's depositors?"

"I'm not sure. You see, I wasn't exactly spending money like a drunken sailor. Literally, every penny I was stealing was going into my foreign bank accounts."

"Do you think he would have written that book if you had told him what you were doing and you shared some of that money with him?"

"That's a good question. I would really need to think about that. There's no way I will be able to give you a simple yes or no."

"Guys," I said, "let's come back to that question."

Mary decided to take a short walk around the neighborhood. She found her way to the park on Cadman Plaza and noticed the all-weather track that appeared to be perhaps a half mile long. She told me she had to resist an urge to do a few laps; it was time to return to the meeting.

When we reassembled Mary said that she was ready to answer Dan's question. However, before she did, she wanted Dan and me to take note of a very important—really the *most* important—explanation for Mike's actions.

"You need to understand that Mike's greatest desire was to write a best-selling novel. He wanted not just great praise and recognition, but to get huge royalty checks in the mail every six months. That was his dream."

"So, you're saying that *that* was more important to him than you, than his marriage, and even his integrity?"

"In a word, Charlie, yes. He believed that after all those years of sacrifice—his, not mine—he craved validation. It would not be enough to write even a highly acclaimed novel. It would have to be a best-seller and bring in lots and lots of money."

"So even if he were putting you in great legal jeopardy," said Dan, "he was bound and determined to see this through."

"Exactly."

The three of us just sat for a while, letting this sink in.

The more I thought about what her husband had done to her, the more steamed up I became. "The man allows you to support him for seven years while he writes a book that almost nobody wants to buy. And then he has no compunctions about stealing your idea and throwing you under the bus?

"Mary, I don't know about you—and you're the one who's calling the shots—but that bastard should be made to pay for what he's done to you."

"Amen!" proclaimed Dan.

A minute later, Mary circled back to Dan's original question: "Dan, you asked if Mike would have written the book even if I had told him about my penny-skimming and offered to share the take with him."

"I think you answered the question," said Dan.

"Yeah, I guess I did."

"OK, then," I said. "Where do we go from *here*?"

We looked at each other. Obviously, there would be no simple answers.

"Mary, I think that while there's no way that any of us could know the answer, may we assume that the reason you came to see me in the first place was because you wanted our help in getting back at Mike?"

"That is correct."

"Mary, since you've been footing the bill, you're going to need to decide exactly how we should proceed. So maybe it would be a good idea to sleep on it. Why don't we get together tomorrow after lunch?"

Chapter 6

The next afternoon we were seated in Mary's living room. Dan asked her to describe her reaction after learning of her husband's betrayal. That and a few other things needed to be discussed before we could even begin to think of what course of action to take.

"I was extremely sad at first. I realized our marriage was over, and that not only had I wasted seven years on that man, but that he was even willing to put me at great legal risk for the chance to write a bestseller.

"It took me a few days just to come to terms with that. And then I began to plan what measures to take in preparation for leaving him. But I was also curious as to how he managed to learn that the information I had on my computer added up to a scheme to steal lots of money."

"How long would you say it took you to find out what you were looking for, and then to leave your husband?" asked Dan.

"About six weeks."

"Did you find anything on his computer?

"No, I didn't look."

"Why not?"

"I couldn't, Dan, because he had never given me his password. There had never been any need for me to use his computer, so I never gave it a thought.

"But what I *did* do was look through his desk when he was away one weekend. I didn't find any pages, but when I looked through the entire apartment I found the manuscript—or, what was about two thirds of what would become the whole manuscript—in a shoebox in his closet."

"Perfect!"

"It *was* perfect, Charlie. And, of course, I had it photocopied."

"I think I speak for Dan as well as myself that this manuscript might be very helpful, one way or another."

"I certainly hope so. But I found something that might be even *more* helpful."

We both looked at her expectantly. She handed each of us a photocopy of a business card.

"Holy shit!"

"Mother of God!"

Mary looked at Dan and asked very innocently, "You rang?"

Dan looked puzzled, so I helpfully explained: "Dan, *think* about it! You said: 'Mother of God' and Mary replied, 'You rang?'"

"Hey! I never heard *that* one before."

I chortled: "Dan, didn't they teach you anything in Catholic school?"

Dan and I were delighted with this piece of good fortune. He was already thinking about meeting with this computer expert—his name was Mark Heigel—to learn what he could about how this man was able to uncover Mary's plan to scam her bank.

Dan then gave us copies of the financial information Mary had given him two days before. He wanted Mary to go over the highlights with both of us.

When she had realized that Mike had to have hired an expensive computer expert, she wanted to find out how he had paid for his services. Going back over the previous two years of credit card bills and bank financial statements she detected a substantial increase in cash withdrawals from their checking account beginning about six months ago.

She concluded that even before Mike engaged Mark Heigel, he must have begun setting aside money. In fact, this was months before their seventh wedding anniversary when Mike asked for just one more year of patience. He was playing her even before he had deciphered her documents.

She had also noticed several cash advances on their two credit cards, which was not just unusual, but went against Mike's normal financial prudence. But since he handled the payments, she had never noticed these items—or that the card balances had not been paid off for several months.

Dan said that by his own reckoning, Mike seemed to have set aside between fifteen and twenty thousand dollars to pay Mr. Heigel.

"That sounds about right," agreed Mary.

"We may be able to use that information down the road," said Dan.

"Now, Mary, let's talk about your decision to leave Mike."

"Once I realized not just what he had done, but the possible future ramifications, I decided that I would leave him as soon as possible. So I needed to begin making arrangements.

"I had been planning to wind down my scamming operation for some time, and now seemed as good a time as any. Also, there was no longer any reason to hold on to a job that I had come to detest."

"So you have had no regrets about giving up such a lucrative operation?" I asked.

"None whatsoever. I have more than enough money to enable me to live better than I had ever dreamed."

I was duly impressed. "You are unique among all my clients. Given your situation, none of them would have had the will power to quit such a profitable enterprise—even if the FBI were breathing down their necks."

It was now past five p.m. so the three of us agreed to break for the weekend and meet again at Mary's apartment at ten on Monday morning. As Dan and I were leaving, Mary handed each of us a letter-sized envelope.

We waited until we were downstairs, out the door, down the block, and around the corner before peeking inside our envelopes. We continued down Seventh Avenue, smiling broadly at one another. Neither of us had ever had a client quite like this one.

Chapter 7

On Monday morning we sat around Mary's dining room table sipping coffee and nibbling miniature Danish pastries. We were ready for the next installment of this saga of betrayal, marital dissolution, and financial fraud.

Mary began by telling us that after having decided that she would leave Mike, quit her job, and actually disappear, it took just a few weeks to make all the necessary arrangements.

She had already secured a new name and Social Security number and had signed an apartment lease. She had also begun the process of winding down her illicit operation at the bank.

"What about your home computer?"

"Boy, Dan. I can't put anything over on you! I replaced it with an identical model, disabled it in case Mike tried to screw around with it, and took the old one to my new apartment."

"Do you think Mike noticed anything?" he sked.

"I'm not sure. Maybe he had sensed that our marriage had ended, or maybe not. But as you guys know, his whole existence was predicated on finishing his great novel."

"Did he have a publisher?"

"No, Charlie, but his agent was going to try to set up an auction among the top publishing houses."

"Isn't that a little presumptuous? I mean, here was this basically failed novelist trying to peddle his next novel?"

"I would tend to agree, but his agent must have been convinced that this one would sell, so she put her considerable reputation on the line."

Dan continued. "So you left work one evening, gave no notice, said no goodbyes, and never went back. And, of course you left all your stuff in your desk."

"That's right."

"And you left all your things in the apartment?"

"Exactly."

"And," Dan added, "you didn't take a bunch of money out of your joint checking account."

"That's right."

We looked at her with great admiration.

Then I asked, "Was your disappearance reported in any of the newspapers, or on the Internet?"

"There were just one or two minor mentions in our neighborhood newspaper. Then, since Mike had gone to the police to report me missing, and the bank also put out the word, I found a few more items on the Internet, but my disappearance certainly did not cause a major splash."

"May I ask what name to use when I look?" asked Dan.

"My husband's name is Michael Jenkins. And I went by my maiden name, Lisa Goodman."

I suggested that since the former Lisa Goodman had disappeared, and that she was now— Mary Smith—Dan and I needed to make sure to continue addressing her that way.

"What I'd like to do—if it's OK with you guys—is a little nosing around for the next few days. Like maybe have a phone conversation with Mister Mark Heigel. Also, I'm going to need a photo of Mike. And if you don't mind, Mary, I'd like to put a tail on him for a few days."

"Yes, Dan, by all means. Give me your card and I'll e-mail you a bunch of nice photos."

"Do you think Mike may be dating someone?" asked Charlie.

"Well, if so, that would be pretty interesting behavior for a man whose wife has recently gone missing. You'd think he might want to find out whether she's dead or alive before he starts dating again."

"What I'll do in the meanwhile is check around to see if he's found a publisher. I'd like to see if the auction actually came off—and if it did, who'll be publishing the book."

I mulled this over for a bit and then asked the two of them, "I know it's premature to talk about an endgame yet, but if there *were* one, Mary, what would it be?"

"Charlie, you and Dan know how much I hate the bastard. But there is *no* way for me to get back those years of my life that he's wasted."

There was a long pause and then she continued.

"OK, *this* is what I want. I want to stop that book from being published."

If the three of us could make that happen, the most important thing in Mike's life would be snatched away from him.

Chapter 8

A week later we were back in Mary's apartment. Mary and I knew that Dan had a lot to report. Before he got started Mary handed him an envelope.

"What's this?"

"Charlie mentioned on the phone that you had incurred a few expenses."

"Well, thank you! But I think this may be too much."

"Let *me* be the judge of that."

"Thank you again, Mary. Anyway, let me begin by saying that I found out some interesting things." He paused, letting the suspense build.

"I had three very enlightening phone conversations with Mark Heigel."

"Which I hope you recorded," I said.

"Goes without saying. I explained to Mark that I had heard from a friend that he had done some excellent work for an ambitious and talented young novelist."

I could not help but smile and Mary just shook her head in amazement.

"You wanna listen to the discs? I made copies for both of you."

"Why don't you just tell us some of the highlights now, and then we can listen to them at our leisure."

"Great idea, Mary. During our first conversation he explained that Mike had found him on the Internet and asked if he could come over and help him with his wife's computer. Mark said he didn't make house calls, so Mike dropped off a zip drive.

"When he mentioned that he charged Mike five hundred bucks to just look at its contents to see if he could help him decipher them, I *knew* the guy was on the take. So I told him that I would be very happy to pay him if he would just explain to me over the phone all the work he had done for Mike."

"Fuck!" yelled Mary.

"Jesus, Joseph, and Mary!"

Dan's face was turning reddish and he had his hands over his ears. But he began to smile.

"Dan, you're a fuckin' genius!" said Mary, hoping she could get still another rise out of him.

I declared: "Mary is one hundred percent right! You *are* a genius!"

Dan continued, as if nothing had just happened. "So, anyway, I sent Mark a money order for five hundred bucks. And then we had our second conversation."

"What did he tell you?" asked Mary.

"Everything! The whole she*bang*!"

"Can you be a little more specific?" I asked.

"Well, I don't want to spoil your listening pleasure when you hear this stuff for yourselves. But I will tell you this: According to what this guy told me, a case could be made for Mary being this book's co-author."

"While I must decline the honor, I truly appreciate the consideration. Now what about the third disc, Dan?"

"Well, I wouldn't want to spoil your listening pleasure."

"Can't you just give us a little hint?"

"OK, Mary, but just a very little one." Dan looked kind of thoughtful, letting us wait.

"Out with it!" I yelled..

Dan smiled. "Fine! Permit me to make an observation. Mark Heigel was worth every dime Mike paid him."

"I think these discs will be extremely valuable. They get to the guts of Mike's crime against you," I said.

"Well, now that we've got *that* out of the way, is anybody interested in the other half of my research findings?"

Mary and I looked at Dan expectantly.

"After *that* performance, I'd just love to see what you're going to do for an encore," she said.

"Well," said Dan, "let's put that off for just another week or so. I think it's going to be well worth the wait."

Chapter 9

We still had more business to conduct. Mary had managed to find out that Mike's agent had had to call off the auction because only one publisher showed any interest. And that just happened to be the one that had given him the $25,000 advance.

"Some suckers never learn," I muttered.

"Well, they certainly won't be suckers if the book ends up being a bestseller."

"That's right, Dan. But it certainly won't be if we do our job right," said Mary.

"I learned that Mike turned in his manuscript, and the book is now in production."

"What exactly does that mean?"

"First, the manuscript goes to an editor who may or may not suggest changes. If there are no major changes, then a copyeditor goes over the manuscript line-by-line, tweaking it here and there, correcting typos, spelling and grammatical errors, and sometimes asking for documentation or further explanation of specific points. The author then usually makes nearly all changes the copyeditor suggested, and then sends the manuscript back to the publisher. From there the books goes to a book designer to be rendered into a format suitable for printing.

"How long does this whole editing process take? For a work of fiction, the average is anywhere from maybe six weeks to three months. When they've all finished, the book goes to the printer, and perhaps two weeks to a month later, it's shipped to the bookstores."

"I guess you've been through the process," I said.

"Yeah. I'm an old pro."

"So what all this means," I said, "is that we still have, say, at least a month to get ourselves into position to do some real damage."

177

Mary smiled at me. "I like the sound of that. What I should be able to do over the next few days is see if I can learn the pub date of the book. What I'd love more than anything is to hit them just after the book is printed and before it's shipped."

"Then they'd get stuck with thousands of copies," observed Dan.

"Let's hope tens or even hundreds of thousands, especially if they think Mike has written a bestseller."

After taking a short break, we moved on to our next order of business, which was Mary's disappearance and possible death. The police had put out a Missing Person's Bulletin, and Mike even got into the spirit of things by posting pictures of her on the lampposts around their neighborhood.

Dan had taken a few strolls around there and had actually caught him in the act. He handed us the missing-person notices.

I then asked Mary why she didn't seem worried about being recognized from the photo.

"Well, first of all, my idiot husband used a photo from eight years ago, which was before we had gotten married. And second, perhaps neither of you guys noticed, but I'm wearing a wig."

"Do you think Mike actually believes something might have happened to you? After all, my guess is that ninety-nine out of a hundred women in your situation would have cleaned out the bank account and packed up most of their belongings."

"Not if they wanted to make it look like just maybe there was foul play. Look Charlie, this way, he doesn't know *what* to think."

"What other preparations did you make before your getaway?"

"Dan, you'll love this one. I took out an extra half a million dollars of life insurance."

It was clear she enjoyed looking at the confused expressions on our faces. Then Dan began smiling and nodding. He had figured out what she was up to.

They waited to see if I would also catch on. They were both smiling.

"Do you mind letting me in on your little secret?"

"Charlie, Mary took this insurance out on her *own* life."

I needed a few seconds to absorb this information and then found myself smiling too.

"Let me see if I've gotten this right. You disappear, Mike reports you missing, and then, maybe a month or two later he realizes that your life insurance policy had been increased by half a million dollars just weeks before you disappeared. That is beautiful!"

"Thanks, Charlie."

"Dan, I can see that you *really* like that little touch."

"Honey, I've been in this game for almost a lifetime, but there's always something new you can learn."

"Thank you!"

But then Dan began to grow thoughtful. Mary watched as his expression began to change.

"Dan, what's on your mind?" asked Mary, in a very innocent voice.

"Yeah, Dan. Spill it!"

Dan gave Mary a questioning look and she quickly nodded.

"Mary has just told us that when Mike looks at the life insurance premium increase he'll know immediately that Mary was not just responsible for this, but also for her own disappearance. She was neither abducted by aliens nor the victim of foul play."

"How can you be so sure?"

"Think about it, Charlie! Only two people could have taken out more insurance on Mary's life—and Mike wasn't *one* of them."

"Of course! How did I miss that?"

"Well, my friend, I do have a couple of theories... but I'm too polite to get into them," said Mary with a smile."

"So Mike now knew two things: Mary was alive and well, and that he better not do anything that might tick her off."

179

"I can't put it as elegantly as Dan just did, but that's pretty much the gist of it."

"With Mary missing, Mike would automatically be a suspect. If the police knew about the five-hundred-thousand-dollar jump in her life insurance coverage—one that took place weeks before she disappeared, then he would likely be the *prime* suspect."

"Dan, you're a regular Sherlock Holmes!"

"You got *that* right, Charlie!"

"OK, gang, what we need to think about is how we're going to use all this information to kill the book."

"I agree, Charlie. Why don't we think it over for the next few days, and see if we can come up with a plan?" said Mary.

When Mary got a chance to listen to the recorded phone conversations Dan had with Mark Heigel, she was completely amazed at how smoothly Dan was able to extract what appeared to be extremely damaging information.

Perhaps most amazing, Mr. Heigel had certainly managed to figure out just what Mary had been up to. And he had apparently very clearly explained her scheme to Mike, presumably using layman's terms. The million-dollar question or—more accurately—the multimillion-dollar question was, how Mike would use this information in his book.

She was well aware that when characters in a work of fiction closely resemble friends and acquaintances of the author, some of them actually sue. In her own case, of course, suing for slander was not only completely out of the question, but it could easily put her in legal jeopardy.

On the other hand, she was growing increasingly infuriated that Mike apparently had no compunctions about letting this possibility stand in the way of his being the author of a bestseller—one that was based on her own ideas.

But she would not know for sure until the book was published. And then it would be too late.

Chapter 10

The following week's conference was at Mary's apartment, where she announced that before Dan presented his encore, she wanted to say something. Dan and I had a pretty good idea of what was coming.

"Dan, these discs are pure gold! While I'm no great legal expert like Mister Goldberg, I'd bet a pretty penny that they may prove to be the heart of our case."

Dan was beaming proudly and I nodded in agreement.

"Thank you, Mary. Maybe after this case is settled, we can send the discs to the private investigators' hall of fame. And now, are you guys ready for my encore?"

We were.

"There's a young woman I've been working with for over a year. She's a graduate student at the City University. I always mix up what she's studying: It's either psychology or philosophy."

"Or maybe *both*?" I suggested.

He had met Carla and had been very impressed. "You'd never know she was a P.I."

"She's a private investigator?" asked Mary.

"Not exactly," answered Dan. "Carla works with P.I.s like me, but she specializes in picking up essential bits of information."

"Is she checking out Mike? Maybe finding out if he's already dating so soon after the disappearance of his beloved wife?"

"So you have your suspicions, Mary?" I asked.

"Look, with the advantage of 20/20 hindsight, I wouldn't be surprised if he were seeing someone even *before* I disappeared."

"*Bingo!*" shouted Dan.

"You're kidding!"

"Not at all, Charlie!"

Mary was totally dumbfounded. "How was Carla able to get this information?"

"From a few doormen."

"That is totally amazing! These guys must know everything!"

"That's right, Charlie! They truly do."

"Did she bribe a doorman in my old building?"

"I believe it was two plus one or two more at the girlfriend's building. Doormen live largely on tips, Christmas cash, and, of course, bribes."

"*Unbelievable!*"

"Not really," I said. "Just a slice of life in the big city."

Dan looked concerned. "Mary, are you OK with all of this? It's a lot of information to process."

"You know, Dan: a few months ago, hearing all of this—especially this business with the new girlfriend—would have been extremely upsetting. But *now*, truthfully?"

She paused for a few seconds. "Now, I feel kind of vindicated. I mean, look what a damn fool I'd been, supporting the bastard for so long. So, yeah, on the one hand, I *am* very hurt. But you know, now I don't give one shit what happens to him. I only wish I could see the look on his face when he gets the news that his masterpiece won't get published."

Dan and I exchanged a glance. We were very glad to see that she seemed to be taking this news so well.

Dan had been hesitating to tell her what else Carla had learned. It had taken quite a bit of poking around. She had spent hours talking to other tenants on the floor where Mike and Mary had lived, especially with an elderly woman who was clearly the building's "busybody."

Dan appeared to be very pleased with how well Mary had handled the news about Mike's infidelity. What he'd said to me earlier was that he thought she might be upset about how very quickly Mike seemed to be going about his normal business, just days after his wife's disappearance. But, of course, she had actually deserted *him*.

Still, he had seemed quite surprised with how well she seemed to be taking all this news. Yes, she certainly was entitled to feel vindicated, but I think he had expected her to exhibit at least some signs of sadness.

Dan had been holding back on telling her something else that Carla had learned about Mike's social life. She might now be ready to hear the rest of this sordid tale.

"Mary, there is one more thing."

"Shoot."

"That woman who Mike's been going out with?"

"Yeah, what about her?"

"After quite a bit of digging, Carla was able to establish a timeline: Mike has been seeing her for two years."

We watched Mary closely, very concerned about how she might react. More than anything else that we'd told her—or what she had discovered on her own—*this* piece of news might be the most devastating.

As soon as the words left his mouth, Dan looked as if he could have kicked himself for presenting this information so insensitively. Even before Mary could register any reaction, Dan was exhibiting signs of shame and embarrassment.

I admit I was shocked by this newest revelation, and looked back-and-forth at Mary and Dan. Dan's face seemed to grow redder and redder. Clearly my friend felt awful.

Mary didn't seem to react at all. She just sat there not moving or even making a sound. But when she looked up at us very briefly, there were tears in her eyes. Her shoulders were heaving. It seemed best to just let her have a good cry—if indeed there *were* such a thing.

For several minutes Dan and I sat there helplessly, not knowing what to do—if indeed there was anything that could be done. Dan shrugged, stood, took a few very tentative steps toward Mary, and then apparently changed his mind and sat down again.

Minutes later I stood up, walked over to her, hesitated for several seconds, and then, very tentatively, put my arm around her.

She didn't react. I wasn't sure if I'd had done the right thing. I could feel her shaking.

Dan decided to leave us alone, so he went into the kitchen. If there was just some way he could have taken back his words.

He tried to recall the saying—something about the written word. Then it came to him.

Pacing back and forth, Dan began to recite to himself that saying which had been attributed to some guy named Omar Khayyam that the nuns had forced him to memorize in the 8th grade: "The moving finger writes, and, having writ, moves on, nor all thy piety nor wit shall lure it back to cancel half a line, nor all thy tears wash out a word of it."

I stood there wishing there was some way I could comfort her. She just didn't seem to be responding. But at least she hadn't pushed me away.

I felt entirely helpless. I was aching to put my arms around her, and to keep holding her until she had cried herself out. That old French movie I had seen, *The Umbrellas of Cherbourg*, came to mind. The gorgeous Catherine Deneuve had starred in it. The movie's story had been about lost love. I remembered just one line of a song from the movie, and to pass the time, began singing it in my mind over and over again: "If it takes forever, I will wait for you."

It occurred to me what a hypocrite I was. On the one hand, I felt tremendous sympathy for Mary. But, at the same time, I was ashamed that I also welcomed the opportunity—however temporary—of being able to comfort her.

Then I felt her hand on my arm. I quickly realized that I had done the right thing after all. It was the signal I had been waiting for.

Dan came back from the kitchen, but then changed his mind and went back inside. A minute or two later, he came out again, tip-toed to the front door, nodded to me, and very quietly let himself out.

A few minutes later Mary began to stir. She slowly stood, took my hand, and led me to a couch. We lay down facing each other. Mary rested her head on my chest.

I could not believe this was happening. I was very happy to comfort her, but didn't dare to even hope there was anything more to it.

Dan had very unintentionally delivered what amounted to a gut punch that Mary could not withstand. Neither he nor I had realized that despite her anger toward Mike—and her desire to be rid of him—he still had the capacity to hurt her.

I would have been happy to keep lying there like this. I tried to think of any woman I had known who had made me feel this good. But there was not even one.

Still, as good as this felt, I knew enough not to think that it was anything more than her letting me comfort her. I continued feeling somewhat ashamed for taking advantage of the situation.

Then I made a bargain with myself. If our relationship never went beyond lying here like this, I would gladly settle for *that* much. As long as I could always be with her.

I now realized that she was finally beginning to go through a grieving process—not only accepting that her marriage was finally over, but suddenly learning that its last two years had been a complete sham. How would *I* have felt, were I in *her* place? Mad, hurt, and certainly feeling very dumb not to have noticed what was going on?

More time elapsed. She had fallen asleep. Still, I had no thought of disengaging myself. Soon I was also asleep.

I wasn't sure how long I had slept, but as I began waking up, I sensed someone lying next to me. When I opened my eyes, there was Mary smiling at me.

"I didn't want to wake you. You looked so peaceful."

I guess we both must have fallen asleep. Was I snoring?"

"No Charlie, but you were talking in your sleep."

"Really?"

"No, silly! So would you like something to eat? I have some leftover pizza in the freezer."

On the way home, I wondered what had just happened between us—if anything more than just companionship. For me, of course, it had been perhaps one of the greatest experiences of my life.

Still, I felt terrible about what Mary must be going through. The last thing she needed now was a guy—especially a guy who was so unsuitable—to be falling for her. Or more accurately, a guy who was in love with her.

Neither Dan nor I had had a clue that at some point she would need to go through her period of mourning. She had lost a great deal over the last few months and had probably diverted herself by concentrating on getting her revenge.

Mary had fooled us both—and probably herself as well—by her concentration on the case that we were building. While I was confident that she would see it through, I was now certain that a new relationship was completely out of the question.

Mary was very grateful, but that was probably *all* she felt. Even after she overcame her grief, there was probably no way she could ever be interested in a guy like me. So how could I even entertain any hopes that she would eventually come around?

Then I remembered what an old friend had once observed after listening to me debating with myself whether or not to call a girl who had given me her phone number. His immortal words were: "I don't see anyone *else* falling out of your closet."

I knew that I was in this thing with Mary for the duration. I had no choice. Great man of the world that I thought I was, even *I* had more than met my match.

I was pretty sure that when I saw Mary again, it would just be back to business as usual. And if there were ever to be anything between us, then I'd have to wait patiently for *her* to make the first move.

Chapter 11

The three of us decided to wait until early the next week before getting together again. Mary would try to check on how far along the book was in the production process. I wanted to consult with a literary lawyer about how we might proceed with the publisher. Dan, who had a few good contacts in the NYPD, learned that the police would probably take more of an interest in Mary's disappearance if they were given one or two promising leads.

Our next meeting was at my office and Mary reported that the book's publication date was just five weeks away. Reviewers' advanced copies had been mailed out a week ago. She explained that reviews would be published when the books were being shipped to the bookstores.

We unanimously thought it best for Dan to hold off on saying anything to his police contacts until I had talked with the literary lawyer. If we acted too quickly, the publisher might cut back on what promised to be a very large printing.

Mary explained that if the publisher were sitting on a huge stash of books—rather than just having signed a contract with a printer—they would have a lot more skin in the game. That would make them much more vulnerable when they were threatened with a lawsuit.

I thought that we had two possible courses of action. One was to present our case for canceling the book to the publisher and hope that the book was killed—even with more than a hundred thousand books sitting in the printer's warehouse.

I explained the second option—an actual lawsuit against the publisher—and very likely, the author as well. This could end up costing both sides hundreds of thousands of dollars.

Mary said that the cost would be no problem, even if the losers appealed. Dan and I looked at each other and smiled. *Those* were the words we had hoped to hear.

We would reconvene after I had consulted with the literary lawyer. Mary then handed each of us another envelope.

Three days later, we met again, this time for lunch at Mary's apartment. "I hate to tell you," said Dan, "but this corned beef and cabbage is even better than my wife's."

"Thanks, Dan. If I ever get to meet her, I promise not to tell her that you said that."

"Now are you guys ready for dessert?"

"Why don't we wait awhile?" I moaned. "I don't know about you two, but my stomach needs a little more time to process that meal."

"I second the motion," said Dan.

"OK then, why don't we get down to cases, as it were. And as the only officer of the court in this group, I propose going first."

For the next half hour, I laid out our case. The literary lawyer had stressed one very important point—that publishers, like other businesses—make all their major decisions based on how they affect their bottom line. If a particular course of action would appreciably *increase* their profits, then they'd go for it. And vice versa.

"In other words," Mary concluded, "no matter how great a book might be, no matter how highly regarded the author, the publisher's first priority is to protect its *own* ass."

"Exactly!" I said. "We need to convince the publisher of two related things. First, if they publish the book, they will be hit with an expensive and very embarrassing lawsuit. And second—and this is a lot more complicated—even if they *weren't* sued, because the author had been less than completely forthcoming with them, they could face even more serious legal issues."

"I really like where this is going," said Mary. "Charlie, is your stomach ready for some dessert?"

"Yeah, I think I'll be able to force myself."

She went into the kitchen and returned with a small cheesecake.

"Wow! You didn't bake this yourself, did you?"

"Of course, Dan! I have this great recipe. It's been in the family for generations."

As she was cutting the cake I couldn't help but blurt out, "Bullshit! This looks exactly like Junior's!"

"Why Charlie, how could you say such a thing?"

"I think he saw the box on the kitchen table." said Dan.

After dessert, Charlie was ready to introduce the plan for their end game.

"What I'd like to do next is draft a letter that will go to the head of the publisher's legal department, with copies to the CEO and the editorial director. In the letter I'll outline three or four general areas of concern about the book."

Dan wondered if they might be curious how I was able to get my hands on a copy of the book.

"Who cares? They'll probably guess that I got it from one of the reviewers. Mary, how many review copies do you think they've sent out?"

"If they're planning for a potential bestseller, then it would be in the hundreds."

"Aren't they afraid that the reviewers will sell them, and maybe not even write the reviews?"

"No, Dan. Even a couple of hundred books would be a drop in the bucket if they're hoping to sell hundreds of thousands. And as far as the reviewers not writing the reviews, I would guess that if one out of every fifteen or twenty reviewers came through, the publisher would be delighted."

"Thank you, Mary. I'm getting a whole education in publishing. Maybe I should write my *own* book."

"Dan certainly *does* have some stories to tell."

"Why thank you, Charlie!"

"Alright, are there any questions?"

Mary raised her hand. "You're not going to present our entire case in the letter?"

"I had thought of doing that, but the literary lawyer insisted that that would be a big mistake. She said you want to kind of tease them, and not show them too much. Leave 'em wanting to see much more. She told me that I should give them enough to make them want to meet with me. Then, at the meeting, I can really lower the boom."

"When you draft the letter, will you run it by her?"

"Yes, but first I want to let you and Dan have a look at it."

"I think another thing we'll need is to draw up a list of issues to bring up at the meeting with the publisher."

"Mary, you're a mind reader."

"Great minds think alike," she replied.

Chapter 12

I completed the lawyer's letter that I would be sending to the publisher and e-mailed copies to Mary and Dan. After getting their feedback, I made a few revisions. Then I sent it off to the literary lawyer.

My thoughts quickly drifted back to Mary, who had become my almost constant preoccupation. I very much doubted that she spent much time thinking about me.

After we'd finished off the pizza that afternoon, I had hoped that she would ask me to stay. But it didn't appear that she would, so I said I probably should be headed home.

She walked me to the door, kissed me on the cheek, and thanked me "for everything."

Mary and I hadn't talked or seen each other until we had gotten together with Dan to plan the rest of their campaign. Clearly, we were back to business as usual.

I knew I shouldn't get my hopes up. And besides, as some ancient philosopher once put it, "Don't shit where you eat."

To apply that advice to my present circumstances, I was eating very well, but never actually got a chance to shit.

Who was I fooling? The minute I laid eyes on her, I knew she was completely out of my league. My chances with her were probably less than of my winning the lottery.

I was still daydreaming when I realized that I had already received a reply from the literary lawyer. It read: "Don't change a word!"

I laughed to myself while thinking: with *my* way with words, maybe *I* should be a literary lawyer instead of an ambulance-chaser.

It was time to start working on a detailed list of things to bring up with the publisher's legal team—*if* they took the bait. I would complete the list and email it to Mary and Dan before sending out the lawyer's letter to the publisher. That way, I'd be fully prepared if and when I met with them.

I decided that the easiest way was to present the items in chronological order.

1. Michael Jenkins' proposal centered on a scheme to skim a penny from each of the millions of deposits made each day at a very large bank.

2. How did he learn so much about bank computer operations?

3. As luck would have it, his wife had acquired this expertise working at a large New York bank for eight years.

4. Did she explain these operations to him?

5. Hand over the three taped conversations that Dan held with Mark Heigel.

6. For the last two years of his marriage, Mike Jenkins has had a relationship with another woman.

7. His wife disappeared a few months ago and there is still no trace of her.

8. He took out hundreds of thousands of dollars in additional insurance on her life weeks before she disappeared.

9. If his wife ran a banking scam and if he participated in the scam, not only might *he* be legally liable, but possibly the publisher as well.

10. The book may provide a blueprint for copycat bank scams.

11. The police will be provided with all this information within the next ten days.

12. Suit will be brought against your company if you do not suspend publication of the book.

I went over the list a few more times, sent it to Mary and Dan to get their feedback, and when they were satisfied with these twelve items, I would send off this lawyer's letter. Then, even if the publisher were to request a meeting the next day, I would be ready to hand over the list.

But I kept wondering if there was something we were forgetting. I went over in my mind what the literary lawyer had stressed. The publisher would do the math: How much will they lose if they *didn't* publish the book and how much will the lawsuit cost them if they *did?*

I began to laugh when I thought how closely what they were doing conformed to Donald Trump's lifelong business model. Trump's companies would sign contracts with their suppliers or contractors to pay fixed sums of money. But they would end up offering to pay just three-quarters of what was owed.

If the suppliers or contractors threatened to sue, Trump's lawyers would tell them to go ahead and sue. Indeed, if they were able to stick it out through all the appeals, they would probably win.

The bigger question was: At what cost? If they sued for $100,000 and pursuing the suit cost them $500,000, they'd end up losing $400,000. In addition, few of the people who did business with Donald Trump could afford extended litigation. They did not have the financial resources that Trump's companies had.

Applying this reasoning, I needed to make the publisher understand that even if they were to win a suit, it would cost them much more than it was worth. Besides, there was no guarantee that Michael Jenkins' book would be a bestseller. Indeed, it might not sell much better than his previous book.

Then I had another idea. I'd order the publisher's Dun & Bradstreet credit report. I once had a friend who had worked at D & B who had mentioned that they had compiled a credit report for virtually every sizeable business in the New York area.

The pub date was getting very close, so I decided to put the lawyer's letter into the mail that day. But I needed the names of the head of the legal department, as well as those of the CEO and the editorial director.

I quickly found the names of the CEO and the editorial director on their website. But as luck would have it, the company did not seem to have a legal department. So I called the main number and asked to be connected with the legal department, wondering how my request would be handled.

I was directed to Mr. Swanson's office. I asked the woman who answered if Mr. Swanson was the head of the legal department.

"Mr. Swanson *is* the legal department."

"I see. Would I be correct in assuming that Mr. Swanson handles the legal work for the company?"

"That would be one hundred percent correct. We downsized a couple of years ago. When the other attorney retired, he was never replaced."

"Thank you so much! The reason I called was to find out to whom I should address a letter."

"You're very welcome."

As soon as I hung up, I had a funny feeling that just maybe the company wasn't doing all that great. I'd have a lot more information within a day or so when he got that Dun & Bradstreet report.

Then I emailed Mary and Dan to give them a heads-up. An hour later three copies of my lawyer's letter were in the mail. Now we were finally in the home stretch.

Chapter 13

The next morning Dun and Bradstreet emailed the publisher's credit report. It wasn't bad. They usually paid their bills on time, and the company did not appear to be in any kind of legal trouble.

The main purpose of these reports is to provide businesses that extended credit to other companies—or were planning to—with a fair idea of how quickly a firm paid their bills and how credit-worthy they were.

This publisher had been in business for more than a century and appeared fairly solid and reliable. I was very pleased that its three latest income statements and balance sheets were included.

It was profitable during two of the last three years. Three years ago, its profits were just over four hundred thousand dollars. Two years ago, there was a slight loss. And last year it made a profit of two hundred thousand dollars.

When I turned to the balance sheets, a few items were surprising. Well over half of their eighteen million dollars in assets were listed as inventory. These were books currently in its warehouse, or on bookstore shelves.

Their current assets were relatively low—just a few hundred thousand dollars. I knew that like most businesses, publishers depended on a steady flow of sales to pay their bills.

This raised two questions. If Mike's book were published, what if it did *not* become a bestseller? Or what if it were not published at all? Either way, the publisher would lose money.

When I glanced at their liabilities, two things jumped out at me. Their total liabilities seemed fairly high, which might or might not be a problem. Among their current liabilities, they had a bank loan of two million dollars coming due in six weeks.

The publisher's net worth—its assets minus its liabilities—was just about two million dollars. And I had a feeling that even *that* figure may have been inflated.

I decided to ask my old friend Moe to take a look at these credit reports. We had known each other since high school. After college, when I went to law school, Moe got a job with a small accounting firm and eventually got his CPA, to which he jokingly referred as his CJA.

When people asked him what the letters stood for, he would reply: Certified Jewish Accountant. Moe was aware that you really needed to be a New Yorker to get his little joke.

Only a New Yorker would know that nearly every accountant in the city seemed to be Jewish. Whenever he encountered out-of-towners, he would patiently explain what the letters C, J, and A stood for. There are probably thousands of poor souls who actually believe that virtually every accountant in New York is a CJA.

I gave him a call, and when Moe picked up the phone and said hello, I asked if this was Moe Feinstein, CJA.

"Do you realize, counselor, that your question is a redundancy?"

"Moe, I am quite aware that any individual with a name like Moe Feinstein would *have* to be a CJA, but I just love the sound of Moe Feinstein, CJA, so I can't resist saying it whenever I get the chance."

"And to what do I owe the pleasure of this call?"

"I just got a D & B on a medium-sized firm, a publishing house that I'd like you to take a look at."

"No problem. Shoot it right over."

"Thanks!"

"Arlene keeps asking me to ask you."

"Moe, when I meet someone, she'll be the first to know."

"Arlene told me to remind you, you're already pushing forty."

"Tell your beautiful wife that I'm well aware of my age, and that I won't even be thirty-six for another two months."

"Why don't you come over for dinner on Friday night and tell her yourself."

When I hung up, I immediately began thinking about Mary again. I knew what an idiot I was to even *imagine* ever being

196

with her. But I was soon fantasizing about showing up for dinner with Mary on my arm and saying to Arlene: "Satisfied?"

After a few more minutes of feeling sorry for myself, I decided to send a copy of the D & B report to the literary lawyer to see what she thought. It can never hurt to get a second opinion, even if your first was that of the great Moe Feinstein, CJA.

By late afternoon, I had heard back from both of them. Moe's response was very measured. At least on paper the company was apparently solvent, although he questioned the valuation of its unusually large inventory. Not all of it would be sold, and those unsold books would have to be written off.

But he was more concerned with the company's liquidity. While he did not know a great deal about the publishing industry, he suspected that the company would be in big trouble if the bank did not renew that loan.

The literary lawyer, while somewhat more upbeat in her assessment, more or less confirmed what Moe had said. But she also observed that while for decades, old publishing houses, left-and-right, had been closing their doors or getting gobbled up by much larger companies, this one seemed to be bucking the trend. Still, financially, it appeared to be "skating on rather thin ice."

That was all I needed to hear. I shot Mary and Dan an email asking if they could make it to my office tomorrow afternoon at two. I attached the D & B reports and my email exchanges with the accountant and the literary lawyer.

Chapter 14

I had asked Mary if she could get there a little earlier because I wanted to ask her a personal question. Mary wondered what that could possibly be. She was well aware, of course, that I had feelings for her and appreciated the great restraint I had exhibited.

When we were both seated at the conference table, I mentioned that she had never talked about her family. Were her parents still living, and did she have any siblings?

She explained that when she was born, her father was already in his early fifties, and he had passed away six years ago. Her mother, who was forty-two when she gave birth to their only child, did her best but wasn't especially good at child-rearing; nor was her father, for that matter.

Her mother, who was now suffering from dementia, was in a nursing home in Albany, and no longer recognized her. She had hired around-the-clock attendants to care for her and was in constant touch with them.

Not only did she not have any siblings, but her closest relatives were her cousin Marie and her husband and young children. They also lived in the Albany area.

She was curious why I was asking her about her family. I explained that if they did not go to court, someone of legal standing might be needed to institute the suit.

"I'm not sure I follow."

"Mary, if we end up suing the publisher, I'll be happy to represent you, but I have no standing with the court to sue them on my own. After all, what personal interest do I have in this case?"

"*Now* I think I get it. Since I've disappeared, I can't very well waltz into court. So you're wondering if I have a relative who might take this on."

"Correct."

"You know, Marie just might do it. If not, I've got several second cousins—whom I haven't seen in years."

"Great!"

Just then Dan arrived. "It looks like you started without me."

"Dan," said Mary, "how could we ever get anything done without you?"

"Yuh got *that* one right!"

We had a lot of ground to cover, beginning with the issue of the publisher's financials and easily reached a consensus that the company was not in great financial shape, but probably not exactly teetering on the brink of bankruptcy either. Still, with just a little push...

Dan suggested that maybe we needed to rethink our strategy. At least tentatively, we had planned to not even threaten a lawsuit until the company had had tens of thousands of copies of Mike's book printed. Maybe that wasn't such a good idea.

"And why is *that?*" asked Mary.

"Well, think about it: On the one hand, they're hoping that Mike's book will not only be a bestseller, but even their ticket out of the financial wilderness."

Mary and Dan nodded affirmatively; I saw that we were all on the same page so to speak.

Dan leaned forward and looked at us with an almost wicked glint in his eye. "But think about what we had been talking about earlier. If we sued them, then they would have just two options. They could agree to suspend publication, which would mean they'd have to eat a huge loss—not just Mike's advance and all their production costs—but also maybe tens of thousands of dollars in printing costs."

"Which probably would bankrupt them," I added.

"Agreed!" said Mary.

Dan continued. "Let's consider their other option. That would be for them to go ahead and publish the book and possibly make hundreds of thousands in profits.

"Even though, in the long run, this trial and the subsequent appeals would end up costing them even more?" I asked.

No one said anything for a while. This was getting pretty complicated.

Then Mary asked, "So you're saying that even if they were convinced they were being sued by someone with deep pockets, they might opt for the short-term gain, while accepting the strong possibility of a much greater long-term loss?"

"Yep," answered Dan. "Especially if they needed Mike's book to go on sale in order for the company to avoid bankruptcy."

"Well," said Mary, "I don't know about *you* guys, but I'd like to take a short break. I, for one, really need to think this over."

I stood and announced that I was going for a walk and would be back in a few minutes. Mary and Dan remained seated.

When I returned, they were deep in conversation. I sat down, not wanting to interrupt.

"Speak of the devil!" said Dan. "I was just quoting someone. I'm not sure if these were *your* words, or those of Adam Smith, the father of economics."

"Actually, we're one and the same. I just look young for my age."

"Then please forgive me," said Dan.

I waited for the punch line.

"I forgot to send you a card on your 281st birthday."

I just shook my head. "Dan, please try to stick to the point you were making when I walked in."

"I apologize," he said, while winking at Mary.

"Remember when you were talking about how business firms make major decisions based on how they affect their bottom lines?"

"That's right! If taking a certain action would substantially increase their profits, they will do it. But if an action will reduce their profits—or cause them to lose money—then they *won't* do it."

Mary and Dan glanced at each other.

Dan continued. "OK, let's consider *this* case: Someone is threatening to sue a publisher if they publish a certain book. If the publisher suspends publication of the book, they'll take a loss on what they've invested in the book.

"Now we come to the interesting part. Suppose the company has already invested $100,000 in the author's advance and production costs. But no books have been printed yet."

"So far, so good," I said.

"OK, so if, under the threat of a lawsuit, the publisher suspends publication they lose $100,000. Now you see where I'm going with this? If we wait until *after* tens of thousands of books have been printed, then the publisher will probably lose much more than $100,000."

I began to nod—and I noticed that Mary was nodding too.

"To sum up," said Dan, "suspending publication *before* the books are printed is a hell of a lot more palatable to the publisher than *after* they're printed."

Mulling this over, we realized that we were in complete agreement: The publisher would much more likely agree to suspend publication *before* printing a shitload of books than *after* they had sunk in all that money.

We each realized that we had been pursuing the wrong strategy. We had a much better chance of convincing the publisher to kill Mike's book before they had the book printed. This way they would not lose so much money.

Then Mary said something that really got our attention. "We know that the publisher is not in great financial shape. It's conceivable that the effort they've made so far on Mike's book might even push them into bankruptcy. Suppose then that they follow the old adage, 'In for a dime, in for a dollar?'

"What happens if they refuse our demand to suspend publication? Well, then Mike's book comes out. Now even if, a year or two down the road the company *does* go bankrupt—or if our lawsuit is what forces them into bankruptcy—well, you both probably remember the lyrics of that Rolling Stones song."

"Satisfaction?" asks Dan.

Mary nods.

I glanced at Dan, and counted one, two, three. Then two of us broke into song:

"I can't get no... sat-is-faction. I can't get no... sat-is-faction."

Mary joined in:

"And I try... and I try... and I try... and I try... "

We were laughing too much to continue. It took a while for order to finally be restored.

"Wow! Three generations sitting around this table—and we're all Rolling Stones fans."

I stared at her with an exaggerated frown, and she stuck her tongue out at me.

"We *both* get your point, Mary," I declared. The only way you *will* get satisfaction is if Mike's book never sees the light of day."

"From your mouth to God's ears."

"Mary, I thought that was a *Jewish* saying."

"Well, you know how it is with the *goyim* when we see something we like, we just appropriate it."

"So what can we do if they decide to go ahead with their plans to publish the book despite our suing them?" I asked.

"We bribe them. Charlie, I hereby authorize you to make them an offer they can't refuse."

Dan and I were astounded. Mary smiled as she glanced from one to the other.

I asked, "Are you *sure* you want to do this?"

"Charlie, I've never been surer of anything in my life!"

Chapter 15

The next afternoon I received an email from Mr. Swanson. The language was quite neutral. But the principals of the firm wanted to meet and looked forward to getting more information.

I called Swanson and reached the same woman I had talked to before. She had been expecting my call and asked if I would be able to come to their office. She provided three possible times they could meet with me.

I decided that I might as well strike while the iron was hot, so I chose the earliest one—that coming Friday at three p.m. I did not expect it to be a very long meeting.

It would take place in the publisher's conference room. I knew all about the home field advantage, not to mention the added advantage of superior numbers. But I hoped that this would not be a contest between adversaries, but rather the first step that would eventually lead to a meeting of the minds.

Mr. Swanson arrived first, accompanied by the editorial director. I explained that I would be giving them some material that pertained to Mike Jenkins' manuscript and to other associated issues that my client thought the publisher should be aware of.

"Excellent," said Mr. Swanson. "I take it that this will be essentially an informational meeting?"

"Definitely."

At that point the CEO breezed in, apologizing for his tardiness. Right! These CEOs are always just so very busy.

I kept everything very cordial.

"We know you are well along in your production process of Michael Jenkins' book and wish to make you aware of certain issues."

I then handed out copies of the twelve-item list, explaining that it summarized my client's concerns about the book and possible courses of action.

"When you've had time to review these items, I will be very happy to answer whatever questions you have."

A few minutes later they were ready to begin their discussion, I handed each of them a large envelope containing the recordings of Dan's telephone conversations with Mark Heigel and additional evidence supporting several of the twelve items on the list.

"These are for you to look at later. Basically, they will support most of the points I'll be raising today."

I clearly had their undivided attention. "Perhaps it would be best to go down the list, item-by-item."

After each of them nodded, I then began presenting my case. Mostly they listened, and occasionally, someone had a question or asked for clarification.

About an hour later, when I had finished, the CEO stood, thanked me for my presentation and apologized once again, but he had to rush off to another meeting.

I had a theory that the more meetings a company held, the less successful it was. Instead of holding meetings to talk about their work, these people could actually be doing it.

After the CEO left, Mr. Swanson got down to cases. He asked, point blank: "Mr. Goldberg, exactly what is it you want?"

"The person I represent has a very simple request:" I paused for dramatic effect. "Do not publish this book."

If Mr. Swanson and the editorial director were at all taken aback, they tried not to show it.

"I see," said Mr. Swanson. "Admittedly this is a quite unusual request. Among other things, our legal team will need to take a close look at these materials."

I was thinking, "Right! What are you going to do—hold a meeting with yourself?"

"You do understand, Mr. Swanson, that time is of the essence."

"*That* I do!" And after exchanging glances with the editorial director, he added, "I think we *all* do."

"Do either of you have any other questions?"

After Mr. Swanson and the editorial director shook their heads, I stood.

"Fine. Thank you both for your time. It was a pleasure meeting you. I think I can find my way out."

Downstairs and out on the street, I replayed the meeting in my head. Did it go well? I wasn't sure. On the plus side, everything was kept very cordial, while neither side gave away very much.

With the exception of a few questions and requests for clarification, I had done nearly all the talking. That was certainly not my usual experience—not just with adversaries, but with most clients. Then again, today I was miles from Court Street.

I had made arrangements with Mary and Dan to meet at a coffee shop several blocks from the publisher's office. When I arrived, the place was almost entirely empty. I grabbed a table in the back and told the waiter that two other people would be joining me.

Mary and Dan arrived within a minute of each other. The waiter quickly brought over menus.

"So how did it go?" asked Dan.

"It's hard to say. I'll tell you what. Let's order an early dinner. From the looks of things, we should have the place pretty much to ourselves."

"According to the menu, they've got the best triple-decker sandwiches in New York."

"Mary, I *do* believe you've become a true New Yorker."

"Is that *so*?"

"Yes! A month ago, you would have accepted that claim as fact. And now, you've become a cynic—just like the rest of us."

"Well, thank you, Charlie."

Dan watched this exchange with amusement. He may have been out of circulation for some time, but he had been around the block a few times before giving up his freedom.

Mary caught his look. If she were just an observer, she might have been entertaining the same thoughts Dan seemed to be having.

When the waiter returned, Mary told him she'd like the Number 3 on whole wheat toast and a cup of decaf.

"Excellent choice!"

"It was a difficult decision. It was between that and Number 4."

"Order both."

"Maybe next time."

Dan and I also ordered triple-deckers, each with a side of French fries. As soon as the waiter left Mary said, "Tell us everything."

By the time I had finished my summary, we were halfway through the meal. They agreed that while the meeting had consisted almost entirely of me trying to state their case—albeit, with barely any mention of a lawsuit—their next meeting with the publishing group, if indeed there even *was* one, would be crucial.

"When do you think that will be?"

"My guess, Dan, is about a week. If they try to drag this out, they'll be running the risk of getting stuck with a whole lot of books."

"Unless, of course, they decide to go to trial."

Just as they were getting ready to leave, Mary reached into her shopping bag, took out two books and held them up. And there, in bold letters, was the author's name—Michael Jenkins.

Dan shouted, "Mother of God!" Half a second later I screamed, "Fuck me!"

Mary thoroughly enjoyed our reactions, not to mention how they sounded in sequence. Dan and I then looked around very sheepishly and were quite thankful that the restaurant was almost empty.

Then I asked, "Is the book already out? Were they playing us?"

Mary didn't say anything, but she was grinning.

"Don't tell me!"

"Don't tell you what, Dan?" she asked.

"Are these reviewers' copies?" he asked.

I let out a very audible sigh of relief. "Holy shit, Mary! Where did you get them?"

"Would you believe, on eBay?"

"Well," observed Dan, "it looks as though Mike just made his first sales."

"And perhaps his last," I amended.

"Well, that might not be completely true." She waited, watching our puzzled looks.

"You see," she continued, "this is such a wonderful book, I'm planning to buy any other copies that might turn up on eBay, Craig's List, or wherever else. But you're probably right, Charlie. Mike won't be getting any royalties on reviewers' copies."

"I can't wait to read what he wrote about your scam."

"Dan, you can read all about it in the last third of the book. *That's* the part I hadn't seen before. I have a feeling you'll find that section very interesting. I will say, the character he created had nerves of steel, very high intelligence and," looking directly at me, "she knew exactly where to find the best pizza in New York."

I was beaming at her.

Dan must have noticed the look that had passed between us, but he didn't let on. Besides, he was very anxious to get into the book.

When I got home, I decided to skim the first two thirds of the book, and then read the last third much more carefully, since it would provide the basis for their case. I certainly needed to be very familiar with the mechanics of Mary's financial wizardry to fully prepare myself when he met again with the publisher.

But I was quickly drawn in by Mike's description of the early years of their marriage, his own hopes and ambitions, and even Mary's sacrifices. Mike had *indeed* stolen her life. Still, I realized that all these chapters were a mere preamble to the central theme of the book: How to steal millions of dollars without ever getting caught.

And then I thought, "Yeah, right! Mary doesn't get caught until this *schmuck* writes a book, and she ends up going to jail. Just the thought that Mike would put her at such risk made my blood boil. This was personal. They had to kill this book!

But then I began thinking of what *I* would have done had I been in Mike's situation. What if someone offered *me* the chance to write a bestseller about Mary's financial scheme, and make a ton of money? It didn't even take a nanosecond to decide what I would do.

Dan, of course, had cut right to the chase. After reading most of the last third of the book, he listened again to the second and third recordings of his conversations with Mark Heigel. Mike had very skillfully described Mr. Heigel's analysis of Mary's scheme almost verbatim. Of course, he did put it in language that the general reader could easily understand.

The next afternoon Dan and I compared notes. We agreed that if and when another meeting with the publisher took place, I needed to make it crystal clear to the gang of three—the CEO, the editorial director, and the lawyer—exactly what Mike had done. His sins went well beyond my twelve-item list.

We decided to concentrate on the specifics of whatever might put the publisher at legal risk. I then called Mary and asked her to see if she could find anything else in the book that might help us make the case.

By the next afternoon, we'd agreed on eight passages that could get the publisher into very hot water. We were now ready to go. I would bring my copy of the book to the meeting and be prepared to cite chapter and verse.

Chapter 16

None of us expected to hear anything for at least another few days, so I was quite surprised when Mr. Swanson called the very next day. Could they meet, say, tomorrow morning?

I decided to drop my customary pretense of checking to see if I could cancel everything in my busy schedule.

"Where and when?"

I immediately called Mary and gave her the news. "Do you think they want to make a deal?" she asked.

"I certainly hope so!"

"Won't the deal have to include their *not* publishing the book?"

"I should think so. But we won't know for sure until I hear what they have to say."

"I wonder what they would want?" said Mary

"My guess is that if they'll give something to us, they're going to want something in return."

"What could they possibly want, besides our dropping the lawsuit?"

"Maybe money?"

"To compensate them for their costs so far?"

"I dunno. Maybe they've sensed that canceling publication of the book could be worth a lot more to us than we've let on.

"Think about it: a mysterious client hires a high-powered attorney…"

When I heard Mary's laughter, I said, "Let me put it another way. When someone is going to all the trouble of trying to cancel the sale of a potential bestseller…"

Then Mary continued for me, "Then just maybe they're prepared to spend a pretty penny… no pun intended."

"Mary, I think you're spot-on!"

"Or maybe they're just very greedy sons of bitches."

"*That's* certainly another possibility. But we're really just speculating. Tomorrow we'll know for sure."

After I got off the phone, I sat there wondering that if it were not money that they were after, then what *else* could they possibly want? Still, it was an excellent sign that they appeared ready to negotiate.

I called Dan with the news. Dan thought that they would definitely want money. The big question was: How much?

I decided to call Mary back. She picked up on the first ring.

"Mary, I just talked with Dan and he seems to think they're after money."

"Yeah, I'm inclined to agree. Listen, it's a beautiful day. How about a walk in the park?"

"I'm on my way!"

When I turned her corner, I saw her standing in front of her house. She was wearing a pair of running shorts and a tank top.

Was she dressed this way for comfort or just to get my attention? Well, she certainly had it! Her legs were tanned and very toned. Clearly, she was a serious runner.

"So, Charlie, where's your running gear?"

"Well, you did say 'walk.'"

"True, but then you would have been prepared just in case we wanted to race."

"Hey, any time, any place."

"OK, Charlie. How about here and now?"

"You're on. Call it!"

"Ready…set…go!"

We took off down the block. A lady with a shopping cart had to jump out of our way. We were neck and neck all the way to the corner. The light was green so we kept up for another long block up the incline to the park.

I drew slightly ahead but Mary quickly caught up again. As we approached the corner, we agreed to call it a tie.

"Not bad for a middle-aged man."

"Not bad for not wearing shorts and running shoes."

"That's why I went easy on you."

"In your dreams."

As we continued walking alongside the park, Mary took my hand. The first thing that flashed through my mind was: Is this a date? Or maybe she was just too nervous about the meeting tomorrow to be by herself.

Either way, it didn't really matter. I hoped we could spend the rest of the day like this.

As we approached an entrance, instead of entering the park, we began to walk around it.

"I've never done this," she confided.

"Me neither."

She looked at me and laughed.

"What?"

"I meant I've never walked around the park before this."

"Oh, right!" I said. Now *I* was laughing.

As we continued around the park, I remarked that I had come here as a kid. "We had a class trip to the Prospect Park zoo in the second or third grade, and I was most impressed with the seals. They enjoyed showing off in front of a crowd. Years later, I wondered if they went through the same antics when people weren't around."

"What kind of antics?"

"Mainly making that strange throaty barking noise and then diving into their pool, sometimes splashing water on the audience."

I then attempted to duplicate that sound, but without much apparent success.

"You mean like *this?*" she asked, and then did an equally poor imitation.

Then we noticed all the people staring at us. Just then, we heard carousel music.

"Yuh wanna?" I asked.

"Sure, why not?"

After three rides, we decided that we were getting hungry. As we resumed our walk, I was very happy when she reached over again and took my hand. Maybe there was hope after all.

Soon I turned to her and asked if it would be OK to ask her a personal question—something that did not have any bearing on our legal case. I added that if she were not comfortable answering, then I would just drop it.

213

My last personal question had been about her family—specifically if she had a relative who could serve as a plaintiff in their case. But now I was pretty sure that she thought I would be asking something about *our* relationship.

"Mary, this is something I've been curious about since you first told me about your skimming operation at the bank."

Boy did she look relieved.

"Sure, feel free."

"You know, of course, if you were to get caught, you would possibly receive a fairly long prison sentence."

"Yes."

"OK, so you were taking a very substantial risk. But on the other hand, there was the possibility of very large financial rewards."

"Of course."

"That's the part I can easily understand. I've have had other clients who, at least implicitly, made the same decision you did—that the risks were worth the rewards."

"Right."

"But what I'm very curious about is if you considered what you were doing was right or wrong."

I knew that Mary wasn't expecting *this* question, and she wasn't sure that even she knew the answer.

"Charlie, I'm not trying to avoid answering, but I wonder if maybe a better question would have been: 'Would you have done it if you respected the bank, and if you had been paid more and were treated better?'"

I started to chuckle. "Isn't saying that like not knowing the answer to an essay question on an exam? And then making up another question and answering *that* question?"

"I hate to admit it, but I have stooped to doing that on occasion—at least in college."

"OK, Mary, I'll play along."

"So my answer to whether or not I would have stolen from them if I'd had a better experience working there is: I don't know."

"Then let me ask you a follow-up question: Would you steal from a church collection plate or from a charitable organization that you support?"

"No!"

"Your Honor, I rest my case."

"So you're going to let me off?"

"No, I'm just a humble lawyer. It will be up to the judge."

Still holding my hand, Mary gave it a squeeze.

We soon came across a Haitian restaurant and looked at the menu posted outside. Even though nearly all the dishes were completely unfamiliar, we went inside. When we were handed menus, we decided to choose random dishes, pretending that we actually knew what they were.

The waitress seemed to be on to us because she was shaking her head as she took down our orders. Then she asked if we wanted some ginger beer.

"I don't drink much," replied Mary, "so could I have just a glass of water?"

"Same here," I said.

The waitress was still shaking her head as she walked to the kitchen.

"I wonder what's wrong with *her*?" I asked.

"What do you mean?"

"You didn't see her shaking her head?"

"Oh well, maybe she can't believe that we don't like ginger beer. Perhaps it's the Haitian national drink."

"Hey Mary, maybe it's really great stuff."

"Maybe, but I've never heard of it."

"Me neither. In fact, I can't remember ever having had Haitian food before."

After a long pause she asked if I wanted to talk a little shop.

"Sure, why not."

"Now I realize that we've talked about this before, but I want to make sure we're in complete agreement."

"OK."

"Remember how Dan was pretty sure that the publisher would want money in exchange for killing Mike's book?"

215

"Yeah."

"When you go there tomorrow, if it *does* come down to that…"

I waited.

"Ask how much they want. Or, if they tell you, then just accept their offer."

I was stunned. Mary sensed that and waited. Finally, I gathered my thoughts and was able to reply.

"Personally, I think they don't deserve *any* money. First of all, they didn't do due diligence. In fact, we did that *for* them. And second, now that they know how evil it would be to publish Mike's book, we would be rewarding their bad behavior."

"Of course, we both know all that!" She paused, and then added, "Charlie, I want to put my money where my mouth is."

"Which means?"

"Which means I'm willing to pay whatever it takes to make sure that this book never sees the light of day."

Just then the waitress brought the meals we had ordered. She looked at us incredulously, and then asked again, "Are you sure you don't want some ginger beer? It goes very well with your food."

"Why not?"

"Make it two!" said Mary.

We began eating. The food seemed a little too spicy hot, but we concurred that it was quite good. Soon I needed to drink some water, and I noticed Mary reaching for her glass too.

The hotness of the food seemed to be cumulative. When we ran out of water, we started drinking our ginger beers. It seemed to be non-alcoholic, and we could really taste the ginger.

"I feel like my mouth is on fire!"

Mary nodded, pointing at her mouth. The waitress appeared and placed two more bottles on their table. As she walked away, we both caught her shaking her head.

As we left the restaurant, I proclaimed the meal "the best Haitian food I had ever eaten."

"I agree. And we ate it at the best Haitian restaurant in Brooklyn!"

We walked with our arms around each other all the way back to Mary's house. As we stood there in the street, Mary leaned in and kissed me lightly on the lips. And then she said, "I'd invite you up, but you have a big day tomorrow."

"I guess we *all* do."

As I headed home I started humming the score from *My Fair Lady*. My first selection was "On the street where you live."

Chapter 17

I arrived half an hour early, so I strolled around the block a couple of times, walked into the lobby, signed the visitors book, and got on the elevator. I was still a little early, but what difference did it make?

When I announced myself to the receptionist, she asked me to follow her. When we got to the conference room, I found the gang of three already seated around the table.

Each stood as I made my way around the table shaking hands. Then I took a seat and waited. The CEO took the lead. He said that each of them—as well as the members of their board of directors—had the chance to go through the materials I had provided.

They had reached a unanimous decision. He then handed me a folder.

Before I could open it, the CEO said that they wanted me to have a chance to review it very carefully. With a nod at Mr. Swanson, the CEO then observed that, "We know all too well how attorneys need to make sure every i is dotted and every t is crossed.

"So why don't you make yourself comfortable in the office across the hall? And when you're finished, we'll be waiting for you in here."

I had no idea what could be in this folder, but they seemed to be giving me the royal treatment. Naturally, this made me suspicious. I opened the folder and saw that it contained just a single page.

I read it three times and *still* could not believe my eyes. I didn't have that much experience even reading contracts, let alone drawing them up. But this appeared to be, as far as I could tell, perhaps the most one-sided contract I had ever seen. I wished I could show it to some of my old law school professors to get additional opinions. Maybe they could even use it for a case study.

The terms were crystal-clear:

1. They would not publish the book.
2. The rights would revert to the author.
3. My client would not sue.

What could be simpler—or fairer? Had it been up to me—even without any previous experience—this is pretty much the contract that I, myself, might have drawn up.

So Mary, Dan and I had been completely wrong. They had not asked for a single penny.

I walked back into the room. They saw by my smile that I agreed with the terms.

Now everyone was smiling. The CEO said, "May we conclude that these terms are satisfactory?"

"They are indeed," I replied, trying to contain my enthusiasm.

The editorial director shot her fist in the air and yelled, "Great!"

Then Mr. Swanson told me that they each wanted to thank me for doing the due diligence that the company itself—and he in particular—should have done. "By calling attention to certain of the author's actions, you may have saved us from being in some very serious legal jeopardy."

"And we also appreciate your bringing this matter to our attention *before* we sent the book to the printer," added the CEO. "We are quite aware how considerate you were to do that."

I was completely amazed at how well this meeting was going. They were treating me as if I were a benefactor rather than an adversarial litigant.

"Just out of curiosity, how many copies were you planning to print?"

"We were planning an initial print run of about 100,000. There had been pretty widespread sentiment here that we may have had a bestseller on our hands," said the editorial director.

"But, on the downside, the author was dishonest with us. And then too, our company could have easily become implicated in a costly financial scandal," said Mr. Swanson.

The editorial director quickly added that there were some other factors, the most disturbing of which was the disappearance of the author's wife. And who knows what else might *still* turn up?

"It's one thing to write about planning a bank robbery, but as you have noted, this book would have provided a blueprint which some reader might have even considered trying to carry out. We simply could not take the risk of publishing that information."

Unable to resist, I added, 'Let's not forget the idiot who might have sued you if the blueprint *didn't* work."

They were all laughing.

The CEO cleared his throat and looked around the table to make sure all eyes were on him. Clearly there was something quite important that he needed to get off his chest.

"Having been with the company since the days we used typewriters, landlines, and mimeograph machines, I have seen the good times and the bad times."

I noticed Mr. Swanson and the editorial director both roll their eyes. They had evidently seen this movie many, many times before. The CEO went on for a few more minutes before he finally got to the point he wanted to make.

But in all the time I've been with the company, our proudest moment, by far, was when our board unanimously approved this settlement."

Mr. Swanson, the editorial director—and even I—were all nodding like bobble dolls. The CEO was very pleased with our reactions.

"We all agreed that this was the right thing to do—even if it *did* cost us some money. Indeed, it is our firm belief that this book should *not* go into print!

Then, looking directly at me, he added, "And we thank you for enabling us to reach this decision. Simply put, it was the right thing to do."

The CEO, who had stood to make his speech, took his seat again, looking expectantly at me. Glancing around, I tried to gather my thoughts, and began by thanking them for giving such careful consideration to the issues that I had raised.

I went on about justice being served, and how impressed I was at how honorably their company had behaved. Indeed, I could not remember a case in which both sides were able to work so well together. And then, I singled out each of them for their contributions.

But there did remain one area of great concern which I needed cleared up. Still, trying to present it as just another thing I was curious about. So I tossed this off as if a complete after-thought: "Let me ask a question: Since the rights revert back to the author, do you think he'll find another publisher?"

"That's an interesting question," responded the editorial director. "Pretty much everyone in the industry knew we were publishing this book. Even though all our employees were sworn to secrecy, the word still got out. After all, in publishing there *are* no secrets.

"That said," she continued, "Michael Jenkins' book manuscript is extremely toxic. I very strongly doubt that any other publisher will go near it. At the minimum, they would be afraid of a lawsuit. But I'd also like to think that our competitors are all honorable people—people who would never consider publishing such a book."

"Let me just add something to that," said the CEO. "If and when people from other publishing houses ask us why we aborted this project, we will tell them why we did. But I doubt that many will ask. I think the word may already be out about the book. In fact, we've just had a couple of queries from the media. And we haven't yet announced that we will not be publishing this book."

I am a firm believer in the old adage, "Quit while you're ahead." So after we'd each signed four copies of the agreement, I stood, shook hands, and left. When I stepped into the elevator, the other passengers saw my beatific expression and smiled at me.

I smiled back. As I stepped out of the elevator I heard someone say, "That guy looks like he just won the lottery!"

As soon as I was out on the sidewalk I called Mary with the news. When she began to cry, I knew how happy she was. I might have been crying too had I been in *her* place.

She finally had gotten much needed closure and I was so happy for her.

"Charlie?"

"Yeah, Mary?"

"Can I see you tonight?"

"Of course!"

I could not believe she asked this. "Would you like to go out to dinner?" I asked.

"I'd love to!"

"Great! Say, I haven't called Dan yet. I'll call you back in a few minutes."

"No, that's OK. Could you come by around seven? Then, you could give me a complete report."

I could not believe my good fortune. Less than a month ago I wasn't sure how I would be able to pay my bills. Now I had just won the biggest case of my career.

But I had also learned that something much more important had been missing from my life. I had always believed in a simple way to test one's priorities. I would ask my friends this question: If someone put a gun to your head and made you decide between choices A and B, which one would you choose?

Now, if someone held a gun to *my* head and forced *me* to make a choice, it would be a no-brainer.

For Mary, this painful ordeal was finally over. She was relieved to have finally extracted herself from a failed marriage and earned what she considered a proportionate measure of revenge against her husband.

Indeed, he had gotten exactly what he deserved. He had stolen years of her life, but she had snatched away his life's dream. While she could never recover that loss, at least she knew that perhaps for the rest of his own life, he would be paying for what he had done to her.

Mary could not get over the publisher's decision. There were still people in this world who behaved honorably. But there was still something that bothered her—something about it that decision just wasn't right.

She began feeling guilty, but she couldn't figure out why she did. She tried to empathize with the people at the publishing house. When confronted with all the facts, they had done the honorable thing.

Although the company was not in great financial shape, they made a very principled decision. They might have asked to be compensated for what was a substantial financial loss. And they did give up their chance to cash in on what might actually have become a bestseller.

Never in a million years could she have predicted this outcome. She felt guilty about having initiated this entire enterprise. While she did not regret for one minute finally getting her revenge, Mary now realized that the publisher might be put out of business.

Was it fair for *them* to be penalized for the sins of her husband—and of course, her *own* sins as well? After this arduous struggle, why didn't she feel better about what appeared to be the perfect outcome?

She might not have cared if the publisher had not acted on principle, rather than just looking out for themselves. And yet, in this sordid tale, only *they* tuned out to be the good guys. But how could she ever set things right?

Then it came to her. She knew exactly what she needed to do. She looked in her desk, found the number she needed, and placed a call.

After providing the necessary answers to a series of questions, and then explaining what she wanted done, she hung up. A half hour later she received confirmation that the publisher's two-million-dollar loan had been paid off in full.

Chapter 18

When I arrived, Mary asked how I would like to celebrate. She was quite amused by the shocked look on my face. I managed to quickly recover and tell her that Dan and his wife, Maggie, had suggested that we all get together for dinner.

"Sounds like a plan."

"So, you're game?"

"Sure, it'll be fun!"

"Great! I'll give them a call and then we can meet in Bay Ridge. They've lived there for years, so they have a pretty good idea of where to eat."

"Hey, do you think they'll know a place that serves ginger beer?"

Dan and Maggie were waiting for us at one of those hipster hangouts that had sprung up along Third Ave. Apparently, they had already started on the celebration.

I was very happy to report on the meeting and its amazing outcome, while the four of us downed round after round of pre-dinner drinks. I had come down from my adrenalin high hours ago and was getting high again just by reliving the excitement of the afternoon.

By the time the waitress took our dinner orders, Maggie and Dan were four sheets to the wind, while Mary and I were not far behind. This had been the most satisfying case of my career and the others kidded me about becoming a literary lawyer.

"I doubt that I'm qualified. Don't you have to read books to get that job?"

Dan chimed in, "Hey, it's never too late to learn how to read."

Then Maggie, who had taken an instant liking to Mary, blurted out, "Yuh know?"

Yuh know *what?*" I asked.

"Yuh know, Dan was right all along."

Mary and I looked at each other and shrugged.

"Don't think I don't *know*. Dan's been on tuh the two of you." Maggie persisted.

"OK, Maggie," said Mary. "*Out* with it!"

"So yuh *admit* it!

"Don't think I didn't see yuh... Yuh wanna know what I saw?"

We waited.

"I seen yuh clear as day holdin' hands under the table. *That's* what I saw!"

"Maggie, it's just your imagination." As Mary said this she pulled my hand out from under the table and placed it *on* the table, with her hand on mine.

"So you see, my dear, you were completely wrong. Where in the world did you get that crazy idea that we were doing any such thing? Why I'll have you know that I'm certainly *not* that kind of woman!"

"Hey, *under* the table *across* the table, *over* the table; it don't make a bit of difference."

Dan was sitting back, thoroughly enjoying himself. The misses sure had a way of cutting through all the bullshit.

"Yuh know what holdin' hands leads to?" asked Maggie.

Dan knew where Maggie was going with this, so he decided to create a diversion.

"I'll show yuh what it leads to!" he said as he leaned over and gave Maggie a big kiss.

Then he realized that the waitress had been standing there all this time. So he made a big show of helping to make some room on the table. As soon as they were served, I ordered still another round of drinks.

Now Dan was ready to make a confession. Or at least he *thought* he was. "I am forced to admit..."

Mary suggested that he try again, this time beginning with, "Father, I have sinned."

Maggie roared with laughter. "Duh you know the last time Dan went tuh confession? This one may go on for days."

Playing along, Dan looked squarely at Mary. "Father, I have sinned."

"How have you sinned, my son?"

Maggie could not restrain herself. "It's about fuckin' time we had some female priests. You *go*, girl!"

"It is a sin that involved money."

"A lot of money?"

"It might be."

"Go on."

Miraculously, Dan was able to almost coherently express his suspicions that the publisher would not agree to cancel publication of the book unless they were very amply compensated.

"My son," said Mary. "You have not sinned. You just made an error of judgement."

Maggie pushed his drink toward him and told him to partake of some holy water.

The waitress was back with the drinks. She surmised that we were not yet ready for dessert and maybe never would be.

"Let me know if you folks need anything else."

"We will," said Mary. And thank you for your patience."

"Hey, it comes with the territory."

"Still, I'm afraid we've been a little rowdy."

"Rowdy? Let me tell you about rowdy. Two nights ago we had a party of eight who were so schnockered, they were falling under the table. Finally, some of their friends had to come by and literally carry them outta here.

"Then, when we were putting the chairs up on the tables, we found this poor guy fast asleep under that same table. His friends didn't even miss him."

"Well," replied Mary, "if we start getting like that, just cut us off and we'll leave very quietly."

"I appreciate the sentiment, but I doubt that it'll come to that."

After the waitress left, I thanked Mary for apologizing for them. Then I started telling them all over again what had happened that afternoon. Dan then suggested that maybe the waitress had underestimated just how drunk we all were—especially me.

Finally, we were ready to order dessert.

"What's good?" asked Maggie.

"Not that much," answered the waitress.

Maggie roared with laughter! "Thank you, honey! You made my night!"

"You know, honey," continued Maggie. "I'm a little older than I look. But I can't remember ever asking that question and getting a straight answer like that."

"Thank you. Now don't get me wrong. Our food is pretty decent, and we don't water the drinks. But between you, me, and the lamp post..."

"Your desserts *suck*!" added Maggie, helpfully.

"*You* said it! Not me."

"So I guess we can skip the dessert," said Dan.

"Good idea!" said the waitress. "But you know that bakery next door? They make the best cannoli in Brooklyn!"

Mary burst out laughing. I squeezed her hand. I was laughing too.

The waitress continued. "Yuh wanna know their secret?"

"Sure," said Mary.

"Yuh gotta eat it when it's fresh. So this place—they do so much business—they put out a new batch every few minutes."

"Are they open now?" asked Maggie.

"Yeah, they stay open late."

When the waitress returned with the check, Mary insisted on paying. The waitress asked if she wanted any change. Mary said she didn't.

Then we all got up and staggered out of the restaurant and into the bakery next door.

After waving goodbye, the waitress brought the check over to the cashier and asked if she could make sure the hundred-dollar bills were real.

The cashier held each of them over a special light, and then said, "These bills are *definitely* real. In fact, they have consecutive serial numbers, which means they're fresh from the bank.

"But this is unbelievable! These folks ran up *some* tab!"

"You're telling *me*!"

Then the cashier said, "Remember how people think that fifteen percent of the check is a good tip?"

"Tell me about it!"

"Well, it looks as though they reversed it. Your tip is about fifteen times the check. I think your tip may qualify for the *Guinness Book of World Records!*"

An hour later, Mary and I were standing in front of her building. She asked if I would like to come up.

I stood there pretending that I needed to think about it.

She let me have my moment. Then she said, "I'll race you upstairs!"

"You're on!"

ABOUT THE AUTHOR

Steve Slavin has a PhD in economics from New York University, and taught economics for 31 years at New York Institute of Technology, Brooklyn College, and New Jersey's Union County College. He has written 16 math and economics books. These include a widely used college textbook now in its eleventh edition, and the bestselling All the Math You'll Ever Need. His short stories have appeared in dozens of literary magazines.